Fergus Craig is a multi-award-winning actor, comedian and writer for television. This is his first novel. He lives 198 miles east of Exeter.

# FERGUS CRAIG
# ONCE UPON A CRIME

SPHERE

SPHERE

First published in Great Britain in 2021 by Sphere

1 3 5 7 9 10 8 6 4 2

Copyright © Fergus Craig 2021

The moral right of the author has been asserted.

*All characters and events in this publication, other than those
clearly in the public domain, are fictitious and any resemblance
to real persons, living or dead, is purely coincidental.*

A CIP catalogue record for this book
is available from the British Library.

ISBN 978-0-7515-8382-3

Typeset in Bembo by M Rules
Printed and bound in Great Britain by Clays Ltd, Elcograf S.p.A.

Papers used by Sphere are from well-managed forests
and other responsible sources.

Sphere
An imprint of
Little, Brown Book Group
Carmelite House
50 Victoria Embankment
London
EC4Y 0DZ

An Hachette UK Company
www.hachette.co.uk

www.littlebrown.co.uk

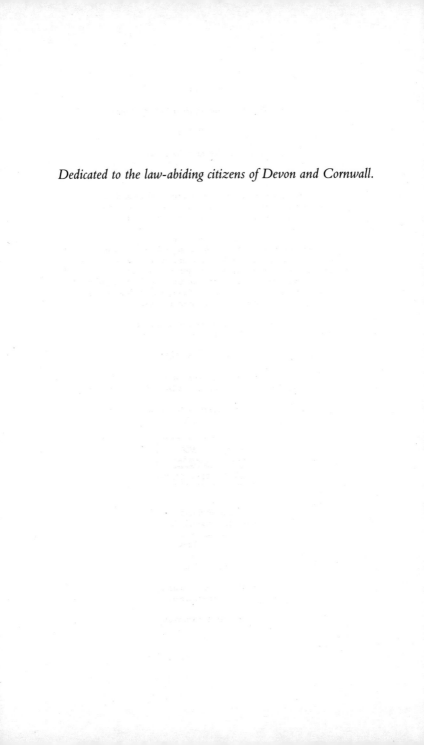

*Dedicated to the law-abiding citizens of Devon and Cornwall.*

# PROLOGUE

A body. In central Exeter, right there in the square. Nothing unusual about that. Exeter city centre was full of bodies. Some were on their way to work. Others were headed to WHSmith to buy a lifestyle magazine. Some were just passing through, taking a moment to enjoy the hustle and bustle of Devon's cathedraled metropolis. But this body was different to all the other bodies, different in one very specific way. *This body was dead.*

# ONE

Detective Roger LeCarre stared at the gravestone with his piercing blue eyes. If only they could pierce through the ground, open up the coffin and bring his old partner back to life. But that was the stuff of fantasy and LeCarre didn't like fantasy, he liked Nazi documentaries and quiz shows and the film *Heat* starring Robert De Niro, Al Pacino, Val Kilmer and Jon Voight and directed by Michael Mann.

Five years.

That's how long it had been since Detective Mick Lamb had been declared dead. LeCarre had argued with the so-called doctors at the hospital.

'Mick Lamb does a lot of things but he doesn't die. *He just doesn't die.*'

Mick's vital organs or what was left of them had said

otherwise. Not that they could say anything – they just lay there in Lamb's lifeless body, refusing to function like teenagers refusing to clean their rooms.

'You're like teenagers refusing to clean your rooms!' LeCarre had yelled at Lamb's heart, lungs, kidneys and liver.

The situation was all too familiar. Lamb was LeCarre's fifth partner to die. Each had met their fate in the line of duty, serving the Devon and Cornwall police force. They all knew what they'd signed up for. When you volunteered to put yourself between the people of Devon and Cornwall and that unstoppable force – crime – there was always the chance you could end up taking a bullet, or in Lamb's case, nine bullets and a moving car.

It hadn't taken LeCarre long to find Lamb's killer: Scott Drink, just a kid caught up in the never-ending gang war between the two counties that straddled the River Tamar, a river that, try as it might, could never keep the peace because it was just a body of water, just a stretch of $H_2O$, not enough to hold back centuries of grudge and counter-grudge.

The Devon and Cornwall police force were supposed to be neutral – Devon and Cornwall – but Lamb had been seen as a Devon loyalist and when he put the Cornish king pin Tristan Trestle behind bars, the boys from Kernow (which is Cornish for Cornwall) wanted revenge. Drink was just a foot soldier earning his stripes. They handed him a pasty and a gun and sent him across the Tamar Bridge to end Lamb's life and effectively his own. Of course, he'd probably be out of prison within a few years for 'good behaviour'. That was how the 'justice' system seemed to work these days. LeCarre often put words like 'justice' and 'good behaviour' in quotation marks. It was a clever way of letting people know what he really thought.

LeCarre had always blamed himself for not being there when Drink had taken out Lamb. 'It wasn't your fault,' everyone had told him, with their eyes. If it had happened any other night of the week (except maybe a Tuesday, which was pub quiz night) then LeCarre would have probably been right by Lamb's side – busting open a crack house in Bideford, chasing a suspect down the A377 towards Barnstaple or just setting the world to rights in the Crown and Goose. That was the life they led. But it happened on a Friday night and Friday night was the night LeCarre always took his wife Carrie for a meal at Zizzi's on Gandy Street. They both loved the way the pizza came out on wooden boards and that was fine – it was a very original touch – but maybe if they hadn't loved it quite so much then LeCarre would have been there that night. Maybe he would have taken those nine bullets himself, or at least three or four of them.

Carrie suspected that LeCarre blamed not just himself but her too. He always said he didn't, but how else could she explain the way he seemed to have looked at her differently ever since his Samsung Galaxy S6 Edge had rung that night in Zizzi's and Sgt Pete DeFreitus had told him to get to the Royal Devon and Exeter in double time? He hadn't even kissed her goodbye. He'd just finished his calzone and left.

LeCarre was married to the force and Carrie knew it. I mean, he was married to her, too. In a legal sense he wasn't married to the force at all: a police force is an organisation and you can't marry an organisation. You could marry every member of an organisation but that would be polygamy, which is illegal under UK law, and it was LeCarre's job to uphold the law. So he wouldn't be doing that and he wouldn't want to, anyway. It would be completely impractical and not even desirable – most of the people on the force were men and although LeCarre didn't have a problem with homosexuality (he'd gotten over that around 2005), he wasn't gay himself and had no interest in marrying one man, let alone five thousand of them. But, metaphorically, LeCarre was married to the force and Carrie was destined always to play second fiddle.

LeCarre didn't blame Carrie but if he were honest with himself, he'd have to admit he'd changed since Lamb had died. Before that night LeCarre was just another cop in his early forties who'd had a few partners die. Now he saw the world for what it was – a diseased sphere, hurtling aimlessly through space, infected with crime. That night LeCarre had declared it his mission to rid the whole planet of crime, starting with Devon and Cornwall and then gradually working his way outwards. Once he'd done that, then he'd have time for Carrie and their daughter Destiny.

LeCarre spoke to the grave, his stubble gently blowing in the morning breeze.

'How's it going down there, champ?'

No reply. To be fair, it would have been weird if there had been, considering the circumstances. LeCarre didn't know if there was an afterlife but he hoped there was. He liked to picture Lamb popping down to hell from time to time to make a few arrests for the big man upstairs. Technically, it would be a pointless exercise as they'd already be suffering the worst possible punishment, but it was a nice image, all the same.

*Five years.*

Five years since the funeral. The emotional strength LeCarre had had to find to deliver the eulogy was still fresh in his mind, as was the standard of the catering, which had left a lot to be desired. He'd written a stern Yelp review that night, whisky in hand, tears streaming down his face like sweat down an athlete's back.

He'd tried to stay in touch with Anne but it was difficult. Looking in her face, LeCarre could only see Lamb and the nights they'd spent together as a foursome, Mick and Roger talking about politics and sport, Anne and Carrie gossiping about soaps and clothes and perfume and stuff like that. Anne had pleaded with him to look out for Junior, Lamb's son, and LeCarre did his best to do just that. Boys needed a strong male role model, especially in a tough city like Exeter.

The way he was going, LeCarre was headed for Detective Terry Gower's record of twenty-two dead partners. That was a record you didn't want to break. He'd sworn never to let another partner die, and so far he'd kept his word.

Detective LeBron Jax was next in line. The boys down the nick had a sweepstake on how long he'd survive – just a bit of harmless fun. No one had thought he'd make five years, but Jax was still standing, all 6 feet 2 inches of him. Or 188 centimetres, as our friends in Europe might say. Jax was black – not that LeCarre had ever noticed. LeCarre simply didn't see colour – he only saw humanity, and Jax had humanity in abundance.

LeCarre had now spent even longer with Jax than he had with Lamb and in that time they'd grown close. Jax had introduced LeCarre to rap music and LeCarre had introduced Jax to the work of Hilary Mantel. In the five orbits of the sun they'd been partners in stopping crime, they'd been through so much together: Brexit, the Atkins Diet, ten to fifteen inquiries into suspicious deaths in custody. Roger was the best man at Jax's wedding and he was still the best man on the Devon and Cornwall police force, of that there was no doubt, no matter what his superiors said in their so-called reports.

'Strange times, Lamby, strange times. We could do with a guy like you on the force.'

The city was in the midst of a crime wave, the likes of which it had never seen, not since at least 2014, anyway. Crime was like a virus spreading through the streets. Everywhere you looked was crime. Out of the corner of his eye right now LeCarre could literally see a woman being mugged, but this was his annual moment with Lamb and he'd vowed never to let anything get in the way of it, so he let the mugging pass. She'd probably be able to get everything back on her insurance – that's if she was smart enough to get an all-inclusive contents insurance. With the range of price comparison websites available to the consumer these days there really wasn't any excuse for not getting good cover.

LeCarre pulled the zip up on his expensive leather jacket, like a forensic pulling up a zip on a body bag. The wind was picking up. The wind of change? Probably not. Nothing ever seemed to change around here. Not really. LeCarre kept putting criminals away, but new ones just came to take their place. Oh well. At least they kept him in work. What if he ever did achieve his ultimate goal of a crime-free universe? What would he do then? Paint, probably. Watercolours. He was an incredibly deep and intelligent man. Think Stephen Fry, but cool and tough and not the voice of the Harry Potter audiobooks.

His phone rang. Chang.

'LeCarre.'

'There's a body in the city centre, by St Pancras Church. Get there now and the case is yours.'

'I'm there.'

LeCarre put his Huawei P30 Pro 256 gigabyte smartphone back into his jacket pocket, the slickly designed curved screen nestling against his garment's lining. He'd upgraded from Samsung to the Chinese device six months ago and had found the process surprisingly simple. If only everything was so easy. LeCarre took out a small green sachet. Time to do the ritual. He ripped the corner with his masculine teeth and poured its contents on top of the grave.

'Take care, Lamby. Take care.'

LeCarre turned and walked back to his car, the smell of mint sauce hanging in the breeze.

# TWO

A pair of eyes looked into a rear-view mirror. The eyes belonged to Detective Roger LeCarre, as did the mirror, as did the Kia Ceed in which they both sat. He didn't look bad for a forty-five-year-old on no sleep. Some wrinkles, some greying at the temples, a little alcohol damage to the nose, nothing to worry about. To LeCarre's disgust, some of the younger lads on the squad were starting to apply premium hydrating moisturiser or whatever it's called. Not Roger LeCarre, no thanks. A couple of years ago his niece had given him a tub of Nivea balm or something and he found himself throwing it directly into the fire just as a reflex. His sister-in-law had said he'd spoilt Christmas that day. What could he say? He was a man and you don't give men moisturising cream for Christmas, not unless you want to watch it burn. He couldn't help being a man. It wasn't illegal. Not yet, anyway.

One thing that definitely was illegal was murder and by the sounds of it there'd just been one in front of the Guildhall Shopping Centre. Time to go to work. He switched off Radio Exe and got out of the car, the silky tones of 10cc still ringing in his handsome ears.

LeCarre had parked on the High Street, a perk of the job. There was nowhere in this city Detective Roger LeCarre couldn't park. He looked to his right, up the gentle incline towards the John Lewis department store. Behind him was Cathedral Green. To his left, the way sloped down towards the River Exe, where amateur rowers would be displaying their skills. A quiet Sunday morning. If Saturday night in Exeter was about hedonism then Sunday morning was about redemption.

Just off the High Street stood the tiny St Pancras Church, in a small, secluded square, surrounded by the Guildhall Shopping Centre. LeCarre wound his way through a narrow side street.

Was there anywhere on earth in which the ancient and the new sat together in such proximity? A thirteenth-century church amongst dynamic capitalist retail temples such as F. Hinds, Claire's and the Inspired Rooms Furniture Store. St

13

Pancras Church, a modest stone structure, seemed almost embarrassed by the excesses of the modern age. Between the church and WHSmith were a series of large steps where shoppers could sit and rest with an exotic burger from one of the outdoor food stalls. On a busy Saturday afternoon, children would run up and down them mindlessly. Did they ever stop to think about St Pancras of Rome, beheaded in AD 304 at the age of fourteen for his faith? Probably not. Too busy pestering their parents for something from the nearby branch of Game.

What had happened the night before was no game. Unless you thought murder was a game. Which it wasn't.

For Detective Roger LeCarre, stepping on to a crime scene was like stepping into a nice warm bath. This was his domain. Tiger Woods had the Augusta National, Roger Federer had Centre Court, LeCarre had police cordon, a newly dead body and some people walking around with those little plastic shoe covers on their feet.

'Sorry, sir, you can't come through, this is a crime scene,' squeaked the young PC.

'Oh, "crime scene", is it? I thought it was a Christmas dinner with all the trimmings.' LeCarre was notorious for making jokes and everyone loved him for it.

The PC stared back. Slow on the uptake, this one.

LeCarre thought of another good joke but decided to let the kid off the hook. He flashed his badge. It glistened in the Sunday morning light.

'Detective Inspector Roger LeCarre, but you can call me Detective Roger LeCarre.' He tended to drop the 'inspector' because Detective Inspector was a bit of a mouthful. Also, just saying Detective rather than Detective Inspector sounded more American which made it inherently better. 'This ain't my first rodeo, but from the look on your face, I'm guessing it might be yours.'

'S-s-sorry, sir,' stuttered the infant PC.

'Don't worry about it, kid. What's your name?'

'PC Mohammed Flintoff . . . sir.'

'How long you been in the game, PC Mohammed Flintoff? You don't look long out of your damn diapers.'

'Two weeks,' said Flintoff.

' . . . for my sins. Say, "Two weeks, for my sins." It just sounds good, trust me. For example, OK, ask me how long I've been in the game.'

'How long have you been in the game, sir?'

'Twenty-four years, for my sins.'

Flintoff smiled in recognition. Sometimes LeCarre gave off a kind of aura and right now PC Mohammed Flintoff was fortunate enough to be the one bathing in it.

'See what I mean?' said LeCarre.

'You're right, sir. Thanks for the advice.'

'Don't mention it. Now, am I gonna do the limbo under this cordon or are you gonna lift it up?'

Flintoff lifted the cordon and LeCarre stepped on to the field of play, crossing himself as he did so. He wasn't Catholic but he'd seen footballers do it and thought it looked cool. He wasn't wrong. He headed straight for Laura Touch, the long-serving crime scene manager and 5 feet 5 inch lesbian.

'Shouldn't you be in church?' said LeCarre. Considering he'd just come from the grave of his dead partner his banter really was operating at a high standard.

'Shouldn't you be in a bloody mental asylum?' shot back Touch, wittily.

Laura Touch: forty, northern, stocky, short hair the colour of the outer coating of a Mars Bar, one of the lads. Laura was the kind of girl you could take home to see your parents as long as you didn't mind your parents being in a headlock. Her job was to manage the crime scene; she was a crime-scene manager.

'Big night last night?' asked LeCarre, already knowing the answer was yes.

'Does the pope shit in the woods?'

16

Touch was what a so-called doctor might call an alcoholic. LeCarre called her a bloody good laugh.

'What are we looking at?' asked LeCarre.

'Young white male. Looks like a stabbing.'

So far, so normal. This was Exeter, the crime capital of East Devon, a place where a teenage boy was more likely to end the day with a knife in his belly than a nutritious meal. That wasn't a fact but it felt like one, so Roger would often say it to taxi drivers. 'Did you know that in Exeter you're more likely to end the day with a knife in your belly than a nutritious meal?' he'd say, before handing them a generous 5 per cent tip.

Exeter – 36 miles north-east of Plymouth, 65 miles south-west of Bristol and, the way things were headed, just a few short steps from hell. It hadn't always been this way. In the Roman era, Exeter was established as a base for Legio II Augusta, a legion of the Imperial Roman Army under the personal command of Vespasian, who was the Roman emperor from 22 December AD 69 until 24 June AD 79 and the founder of the Flavian dynasty. In the Middle Ages, Exeter became a religious centre, with Exeter Cathedral built in the mid-eleventh century, going on to become Anglican in the sixteenth-century English Reformation. In the late nineteenth century, Exeter became an affluent centre for the wool trade before the post-war rebuilding led it to become a centre for tourism and business in Devon and Cornwall. LeCarre was a keen history buff and had read most of Wikipedia.

So what changed? Drugs. When LeCarre was a kid, if you'd said the word 'drugs', he wouldn't have known what you were talking about. It'd just have been a meaningless sound to him like 'gik' or 'trotch'. If you said the word 'drugs' to an Exeter eight-year-old now you'd probably get a 'yes please' and a 'what have you got?' tumbling out of their not-so-innocent mouth. Drugs first hit the partially cobbled streets of Exeter in the mid-1990s. Touring Britpop bands were to blame. They arrived with catchy tunes sung by drugged-up loons and left chumps like LeCarre to clean up the mess.

He never understood the appeal. Why stick powder up your nose when you can stick Southern Comfort and lemonade down your throat? His wife thought he drank too much. Yeah, well, he thought she talked too much. Especially when he was watching his quiz shows. LeCarre had seen every episode of *University Challenge* and never got an answer wrong except on one occasion when Paxman asked a question about some American 'rapper' called Nicki Minaj which should never have been on a high-end quiz show like *University Challenge*, so didn't really count.

From the wool trade to the drugs trade. Talk about a

city in decline. LeCarre ran 10 kilometres most days but he probably burned the most calories just from shaking his head at what had become of his town. At least it kept him trim. Not like Laura Touch, his roly-poly colleague.

'Do we have an ID?' asked LeCarre, using the police lingo for identification.

'Kid called Charlie Fade. Nineteen. No one's spoken to the family yet. The body's still here if you wanna take a look.'

'Why go to the theatre if you don't wanna see the show, right?' said LeCarre. 'Who found him?'

'Jogger by the name of Cindy Squire, found him at six a.m.'

Joggers were always finding bodies.

'Any sign of Jax?'

'Couldn't make it. Dentist appointment. Looks like you're flying solo for now,' said Touch.

Dentist appointment? On a Sunday? Jax had the healthiest-looking teeth LeCarre had ever seen. *Interesting.*

'Catch you later, Touch.'

LeCarre could see the body boffins doing their science around the adolescent corpse. He walked over with the nonchalance of a man being led to his table in Café Rouge or Pizza Express or Frankie & Benny's. What you have to understand is that this was an everyday thing for Roger

LeCarre. The way you look at a tube of toothpaste? That's how LeCarre looked at a corpse. The way you look at a stapler? That's how LeCarre looked at a corpse. Or a pair of black socks? Or a kitchen cupboard with some carrier bags in it? That's how LeCarre looked at a corpse. Do you see what I'm getting at? Every day. Like a tuna-melt panini or a receipt from a well-known supermarket – that's how Detective Roger LeCarre looked at a corpse.

'Oh look, it's the three amigos,' said LeCarre humorously.

Des Hamilton, Todd Hendrix and Max Trescothick were three of the best forensics this side of Bristol. It was good to know they were on the job.

'Morning, LeCarre,' said Trescothick.

'Can I take a look?'

'Be my guest.'

And there he was. Charlie Fade. He looked almost peaceful, like he was relaxing in a pool of chlorinated water at a five-star resort, rather than a pool of his own blood. He lay in front of the little church's entrance. Something unholy had occurred on God's doorstep. Perhaps God had witnessed it. If God was omnipresent then He was a witness to every murder and yet to LeCarre's continual irritation it was impossible to get Him to testify in court – an undeniable flaw in the justice system.

'Who killed you, Charlie?' asked LeCarre, pointlessly. He turned to Trescothick. 'Anything worth mentioning?'

'Stab wound, lost a lot of blood. Died late last night, I would have thought, but Gita will have to confirm that.'

LeCarre crouched down and put his rugged hand to his chin. There was never a second opportunity to see a crime scene for the first time. For a murder detective, this was a key moment.

'Soak it in, Rog. Soak it in,' LeCarre whispered to himself.

Nineteen years old. Poor kid. He should have been running around town, not being dead around town.

Nineteen.

At nineteen Roger LeCarre was a new police officer, a young pup on the Bodmin beat. Life was just getting exciting; he didn't have time to get killed, there was too much to learn. Back then, LeCarre was a sponge. He wanted to know everything there was to know about being a good police officer – investigation, interrogation, undercover work. He was a good little recruit who did things by 'The Book'. The Book. Who wrote The Book, anyway? Certainly not someone who'd ever done any real police work, that was for sure.

One day Roger would write his own book, one that could be handed to every new recruit on their first day on the force. It would be one page long and all it would say is: 'Stop reading this bloody book and get your arse out on the streets, dammit.'

He didn't have time to write books right now, though. There was a murder to solve.

LeCarre stood up and paced around the body, taking it all in, like an art enthusiast staring at a picture by Picasso or Monet or Rembrandt Harmenszoon van Rijn – or Rembrandt for short. Being incredibly deep, Roger was no stranger to the world of art, but for him, nothing came close to the gothic beauty of a cadaver on concrete.

'Stick that in a gallery,' he said to himself, weirdly.

He'd seen a thousand dead bodies in his time. The question was, what was different about this one? There must be a clue somewhere, something nobody else had spotted. There always was. That was LeCarre's job – to see things others didn't see.

He started at the feet. A pair of black Nike Air Max trainers. Trainers suggested Fade liked his sport. LeCarre leaned in. The tread on the right foot was more worn than the tread on the left. So Fade had a limp, of that there was no doubt. A sports injury? Could have made it harder to run from his attacker. Perhaps he'd sprained his ankle in a five-a-side football match, had been out of the team for a while

22

and was now on his way to recovery, but the person who'd replaced him in the team didn't want to be dropped from the side for a fit Charlie Fade so had killed him the night before their next game. LeCarre couldn't be sure yet but it was a good theory. If Jax ever showed up, Roger could send him to interview all the Sunday League players in the area. It was certainly an avenue worth pursuing.

LeCarre's investigative eyes moved to Charlie Fade's legs and the blue jeans in which they lay. Jeans and trainers. As LeCarre knew only too well, all of Exeter's nightclubs ran a strict no caps, no jeans, no trainers policy – the no blacks, no dogs, no Irish of the twenty-first century. So here was a nineteen-year-old lad, out on a Saturday night but with no intention of going to a nightclub. There was only one explanation: Charlie Fade was a real-ale fanatic.

Roger extrapolated in his mammoth mind – young Charlie Fade had started the evening with a friend. They'd gone from pub to pub to pub to pub. The Crown and Goose, the Farmer's Union, the Ship Inn, the list goes on, a pint of best in each, the *Good Beer Guide* in hand. Being young men, they'd been cavalier with the ABV (or alcohol by volume). Rather than sticking to beers with an ABV of below 4 per cent, they'd recklessly just picked whatever beer they fancied, whichever beer's pump had the prettiest label.

By 10 p.m., all inhibitions had gone and they'd started to argue. Charlie had told his friend some home truths, truths about their time at school together, truths his friend didn't care to hear. They'd taken their dispute out on to the street but Charlie didn't account for his friend's knife – a knife which found its way into his ale-sodden guts.

LeCarre already had two very strong theories on Charlie Fade's murder and his gaze hadn't even got as far as Fade's knees yet.

Now it was time to look at the business end – Charlie Fade's blood-covered torso. Roger had the stomach for it, even if poor Charlie didn't, not any more.

A red jacket, red from blood, a deep red, like the £9 bottle of Malbec LeCarre had drank the night before as he'd prepared himself to visit the grave of his dead partner Mick Lamb. But this jacket hadn't started last night Malbec red. The blood hadn't quite made its way to Fade's shoulders. There, the jacket was green. To an outsider that might mean nothing. Green like grass, green like American money, green like the baize on a freshly cut snooker table. Green. So what? But in Devon and Cornwall? You don't wear green by accident.

Green.

*Green like the flag of Devon.*

Of course, there's nothing unusual about a Devonian wearing his county's colour with pride. What it did was identify him as a member of a tribe, a young man loyal to a county which went back thousands of years and to its flag, which dated back to 2006 when it was first adopted by Devon County Council after a web poll. Was there a Cornishman out in Exeter last night? If so, we had our chief suspect. That green jacket could have served as a red rag to a bull. The most obvious thing would be to close the Tamar Bridge immediately, lock every Cornishman up and interrogate them until one of them cracked.

LeCarre's superiors and their beloved red tape wouldn't allow it. He knew that, no point even asking. Oh well. He'd have to solve this crime the hard way.

And now to take a look at Charlie Fade's dead face. Nothing remarkable. A nose, a mouth, a chin. Once you'd seen one face you'd seen them all.

But his eyes. They seemed to look directly into LeCarre's own and in that moment they seemed to say something.

'Solve my murder, Detective Roger LeCarre. Solve my murder, please. Bring my killer to justice.'

'I'll do my best, Charlie,' replied LeCarre. 'I'll do my best.'

High up above, an eye looked down on the detective.

A CCTV camera. Another set of eyes watched a monitor, watched LeCarre.

'Don't solve his murder. Don't bring his killer to justice,' whispered a voice. 'Because his killer is me. *I killed Charlie Fade.*'

# THREE

Four alloy wheels travelled down a road at 57 miles per hour. They were the wheels of Detective Roger LeCarre's 2018 Silver Frost Kia Ceed, which he was currently driving. The agile and robust five-door hatchback offered LeCarre an intriguing blend of power, comfort and reliability. The 1.4-litre engine gave him affordable fuel economy while Kia's Flex Steer system provided an ease of handling he could trust. A simple yet stylish interior coupled with front seat lumbar support adjustment added comfort and luxury – this was his cocoon from the rigours of the outside world. His Ceed was sexy but safe and like all safe sex, low on carbon emissions. LeCarre didn't expect to use the seven-year warranty but, like the taser gun strapped to his leg, it was nice to know it was there. At home in both the city and the countryside, whenever he was behind the wheel of his Kia

Ceed, LeCarre felt confident that he could navigate all that Devon and Cornwall threw at him.

Turning his three-spoke multifunction steering wheel, LeCarre changed lanes. He was headed towards Exeter's Westside, the rougher part of town, west of the Exe. LeCarre braced himself as he crossed the river. Familiarity with the districts of St Thomas and Exwick went with the job but familiarity bred if not contempt then a cautious, grudging respect for the menace they housed.

'So I'm a solo artist now, huh? Like Elton John or Joni Mitchell or . . . what's that young guy the kids are all listening to? Oh yeah, the Brit Award-winning Lewis Capaldi.'

LeCarre was gently ribbing his partner LeBron Jax through the medium of a Bluetooth connection to his 7-inch touch-screen infotainment system. He was savvy enough to have a phone tariff with unlimited minutes so this conversation wasn't costing him a dime, but knowing Jax was squirming was worth every goddamn penny.

'Dentist appointment? On a Sunday? Brother, you gotta come up with a better excuse than that.'

'You got me,' said Jax. 'You got me good.'

'Please tell me she was worth it.'

'She?'

'Oh, come on. Don't take me for a fool like Joey Tribbiani

from *Friends* or Trinculo the fool from Shakespeare's masterpiece *The Tempest*. I'm just your work wife, buddy, not your real one. She must have been a damn fine piece of tail to keep you away from a brand new murder scene.'

Some wouldn't care for it but this was just the unvarnished way coppers spoke to each other on the Devon and Cornwall police force. They spoke like men.

'A gentleman never tells, LeCarre, surely you know that?'

'Oh, so you're a gentleman now, huh?' Roger let out a large manly chuckle. 'Well, that's news to me, pal.'

'Word on the street is I'm not the only one who didn't spend last night in the marital bed.'

A brief, uncomfortable pause.

'I thought I told you, Jax.'

'Sorry, LeCarre, I forgot. The anniversary of Lamb's death.'

LeCarre had spent the night before doing what he always did the night before a visit to the grave of a dead partner – staying in a nearby Premier Inn and drinking himself into oblivion. Carrie didn't need to see his grief pit, so he never let her in. Premier Inn plus alcohol – that's how he dealt with these things. He felt cleansed now. That's what a Tesco Finest Malbec, a few whiskies and a £2 KitKat chunky from the mini bar could do.

'Don't worry about it, Bron. I'm just glad you got laid.'

Adultery was a part of life for a Devon and Cornwall police officer. It wasn't pretty but it was the truth. You couldn't see the things you saw every day on the streets of Redruth or Plymstock or Paignton and not find a vice to ease the pain. Some chose alcohol, some chose sex, some chose KitKat Chunkies. Most chose all three. Staying faithful to your wife wasn't made easier by the fact that a Devon and Cornwall police badge seemed to be the most powerful aphrodisiac around. Women were attracted to the danger it implied. Coppers didn't write the rules but they weren't shy about taking advantage – and who could blame them? Their wives, no doubt.

'So who's the unlucky guy?' said LeBron.

'Huh?'

'The body.'

Oh yeah, the body.

'Charlie Fade. Nineteen years old.'

LeCarre could hear the sound of Jax shaking his head in sadness.

'You know him?' asked LeCarre.

'One of Donkey's boys.'

Donkey Malone. Exeter drug lord, scourge of the Devon and Cornwall police force, known from Bideford to Bodmin. A specialist in crime.

LeCarre was still keen on his real ale-based theory but this new information did seem to open things up a little.

'You knew him well?'

'Not well. Looked like a good kid, though.'

'Good kids don't work for Donkey Malone, Jax. You know that.'

'True. So what's the plan?'

'Tomorrow, we'll go down to the ghetto. Crack some heads together – see if any clues fall out.'

'And what about now?'

'I've got something else to break.'

'Oh yeah? What's that?'

'News.'

# FOUR

The small metal object rotated the liquid like an Oklahoma tornado. The object was a spoon and the liquid was tea. A cup of tea made for Detective Roger LeCarre. Its maker? Melanie Fade.

LeCarre admired her curvaceous curves. She looked like Michelle Pfeiffer but younger and with bigger breasts. It was such a shame he had to tell her that her son was dead.

LeCarre looked around. Melanie's house was a three-bedroomed semi-detached in one of Exeter's less salubrious suburbs. Probably worth about £130,000 but he'd check on Zoopla later. Pink walls, silk cushions, an elegant chaise longue – the place had a woman's touch.

'Have you come far, officer?' she asked.

'I was just in the centre of town. Took the A377 but it's

a Sunday so the traffic wasn't too bad. Took about, ooh, fifteen minutes?'

'Oh that's not too bad. Traffic can be an absolute nightmare going in on a weekday.'

'Yeah, it's the one-way system. Also, the timings on the traffic lights are all wrong,' proffered LeCarre, intelligently. 'You can find yourself sat on red for ten minutes and that's no good to anyone. Someone needs to tell the council that traffic lights are supposed to control traffic flow, not stop it altogether.'

'You're not wrong there, Officer. What were you doing in town? Nothing bad's happened, I hope?'

'I think you better sit down.'

Melanie Fade walked her attractive body to a chair and placed her shapely posterior on the upholstery.

'Have you got that tea?' asked LeCarre.

'Oh yes. Sorry, officer. My mind's all over the place.'

She got up, went back to the kitchen, got LeCarre's cup of tea, handed it to him and sat down again, sexily.

'Your son's dead.'

Telling a mother her son was dead was the worst part of a copper's job. That and paperwork. All the lads on the force hated paperwork and telling mothers that their sons were dead.

'Ricky?'

'No, the other one.'

'Not Robbie?'

'Other one?'

'Charlie?'

'Yeah, that's the one. Charlie.'

A single tear rolled Melanie's face. LeCarre followed it with his eyes as it fell off her face and landed on one of her breasts.

These days the force was very keen on training in the workplace, courses on how to do this or that. LeCarre thought it was all bullcrap. There'd been one a couple of weeks ago called 'grief sensitivity'. Roger and LeBron skipped it and went ten-pin bowling. 'You don't learn good police work on a course.' LeCarre was fond of spitting the word 'course' out with the disrespect it deserved. 'Course! Ha!' Good police work was about the gut, acting on instinct. Nothing you could learn on some course.

'What . . . what happened?' she asked.

'Stabbed. There was a lot of blood. You should have seen it. Mental.'

'Why? Oh my God! Who?'

She was really crying now, like an Oscar-winning actress in a good film, except this crying was different – this crying was real.

'I'm afraid we don't know who did it – not yet, anyway. I was hoping you could tell me a little bit about Charlie.'

LeCarre thoughtfully handed her a box of tissues. Melanie Fade took one and wiped the tears from her face and breasts.

'Yes, yes of course.' The sexy woman steadied herself. 'He was such a sweet little boy. Always used to help out in the kitchen – Mummy's little helper, I'd call him—'

'Can you skip forward a bit? Don't really need to know anything pre-pubes.'

'Sure. Things started to go wrong when his father went to prison. I married badly, I can admit it now. They say women can't resist a bad man – well, I'm very much a woman, Detective.'

'I couldn't help but notice,' said LeCarre fiendishly.

'Wade always said he was going to go straight. I blame this rotten city, this nest of vipers. It just kept dragging him down.'

'There is always a choice, Ms Fade. One can choose not to do crime.'

'You're right, Officer, of course you are.'

'What did he go down for in the end?'

'Go down' was street lingo for going to prison.

'Selling counterfeit perfume.'

'THE BASTARD!' LeCarre banged his fist against her

rectangular coffee table. Such was his conviction, that just hearing about a crime could send LeCarre into a rage. Sometimes this made his job as a police officer difficult.

'With Wade locked up ... well, some boys need a male role model, you know? Charlie went looking and unfortunately he found one.'

'Donkey Malone.'

'You know Donkey?'

'Does Albert Einstein know the square root of sixty-four? I'm a Devon and Cornwall police officer – yeah, I know Donkey Malone. Let's just say he's good for business. If your business is crime or, in my case, stopping crime ... that is to say, being the city's biggest crime boss, he provides me with a lot of crime to investigate, which you could say is good for my business, the business of police work, although obviously ultimately I'd prefer it if there wasn't any crime at all so I could concentrate on something else like painting watercolours or learning to play the piano.'

'Biscuit?'

'Thank you.'

Melanie Fade passed him a plate with some custard creams on it, sexily.

'Charlie ... I'm telling you, Detective, he was such a

lovely boy, but he started hanging around with the wrong kids. Shoplifting, doing drugs . . . '

That word. *Drugs*. LeCarre clenched his fist, tightly. Melanie Fade continued.

'I can't say I didn't notice a change in him. I tried to get through to Charlie, tell him he was headed in the wrong direction. I don't know if you have children yourself but, you know how they are, he didn't want to listen.'

'Was Charlie *working* for Donkey Malone, do you know?'

There was a kind of shame in Melanie Fade's face. Like a dog who'd just defecated on the carpet. But this was the most attractive defecating dog Roger LeCarre had ever seen.

'Yes. Yes, I think so, Officer. He certainly seemed to have a lot more money. He was proud of it – started wearing designer clothes, shopping at Waitrose, set up a pension plan. You know teenagers, boys will be boys.'

'Was he dealing? Was he dealing drugs? Drugs, Ms Fade – do you think Charlie was dealing drugs?'

Each time LeCarre said the word 'drugs' he said it with a deeper intensity, a stronger venom, a venom that expressed the misery that drugs brought everywhere they went – except for drugs like alcohol and caffeine and the sort of drugs you got at the chemist like Lemsip, stuff like that.

'I don't know, Detective. I guess I was looking the other

way. Probably? He was a good boy. He really was, very proud of his Exeter roots.'

LeCarre fixed her with his masculine eyes.

'And yet he was pushing the very thing that's destroying this city.'

Melanie put her head into her attractive hands.

'He was my youngest. The other two, they're older, left home. But he was my special little boy and now he's gone. It's just me now, I'm all alone.'

LeCarre placed his attractive hand on her attractive knee. 'You're not alone now.'

Detective Roger LeCarre had never made love on a chaise longue before. He had done so on a sofa, a swivel chair, a church pew, a sort of banquette, an armchair, a slide at an adventure playground, the back seat of a car, an inflatable mattress and, obviously, a number of beds, but never a chaise longue – not until now. LeCarre often ran through the different types of furniture he'd had penetrative sex on as a method of delaying climax and right now it was working. Oh, it was working. He looked at his expensive watch. They'd been making love for roughly fifty-five minutes so far, nearly an hour if you included the foreplay – not bad.

LeCarre ran his hand down Melanie Fade's incredible

body, starting at her forehead. She was in fantastic shape – the shape of a woman. She was sitting on top of him, her head swirling round in a clockwise direction, just like the spoon in the tea, the one from earlier on. Her wild brown hair was flung from side to side, her face displaying the ecstasy powering through her body. For a woman who'd just heard her son was dead she was having a terrific time.

This was what sex with Roger LeCarre could do – it could transport you somewhere else, away from whatever was troubling you. He was a Boeing 737 and if you were lucky enough to have a ticket, he'd take you to where you wanted to go – first class.

He looked at his watch again. One hour. He should probably get going, really. Sex could ease her pain but only in a temporary, superficial way. The only thing that could truly heal her grief was justice and Detective Roger LeCarre was the man to provide it. As much as he'd like to, the simple truth was he couldn't find her son's killer with his proud length (his penis) inside of her.

*Unless she was her son's killer?*

Probably not. Seemed unlikely.


Melanie Fade led LeCarre to the front door. Her silk dressing gown hid her body but not its satisfied glow. She kissed him tenderly on the cheek then opened the door, letting in the Devonian sunlight.

'If you're heading back into town you're best off going that way. There's roadworks on Ashpole Way.'

'OK, thanks,' said LeCarre, walking to his award-winning Kia Ceed.

'Oh, and Detective LeCarre?'

'Yes?'

'You will find Charlie's killer, won't you?'

LeCarre looked into her grief-ridden but also stunning face one last time. 'Don't worry. I always do.'

'Is that a promise?'

'Yes. It's a promise. *I promise to find your son's killer.*'

# FIVE

The light slowly faded from the famous Exeter skyline and the city grew dark because it was no longer daytime – it was something else. Something ominous. Something grim. Something that had happened many times before and would no doubt happen again: evening, about 8 p.m.

Filled with forebodings of darker times to come, the moon shone down on Rougemont Castle, a thousand-year-old monument to Exeter's troubled history and also a premier hospitality venue. The great and the good of East Devon were gathered. The great and the good ... and no doubt some of the bad. The castle's ballroom was filled with circular tables and highly trained waiters serving elegant wine. It looked like the Golden Globes except everyone was from Exeter.

Jimmy Spindle, Exeter City Football Club captain, was

there with his beautiful Instagram-star girlfriend Prosecco Rashid. Black tie and evening gown wasn't their usual attire but they looked happy enough to be amongst the city's elite. Also in attendance were faces from the world of entertainment – Radio Exe's cheeky breakfast duo Kelly and Baz sat at a table with presenters from BBC Southwest regional programme *Spotlight* and popular local racist comedian and sometime panto dame Cosmo. Representing the world of business was plumbing billionaire Terrance Pike, jewellery magnate Peter Tharrington and Clinton Cards heiress Tabitha Cynch. Local MPs, councillors, influential lawyers and members of the clergy. The president of the Exeter Freemasons. It was quite the occasion.

Detective Roger LeCarre looked around. If a bomb went off tonight . . . it didn't bear thinking about. Not least because he was sitting with his wife Carrie and his brothers in arms from the Devon and Cornwall police force. Unusually, their table was near the front of the room – someone must have done somebody a favour. LeBron was there, leaning back, puffing on a Cuban vape beside his dyslexic wife Jackie. Detective Inspector Todd Gatting and Detective Inspector Rico Hernandez were sharing a joke, while their wives rolled their heavily made-up eyes. Chief Superintendent Beverley Chang was the only copper without a spouse for company. Did she have one? LeCarre didn't even know. For all his detective skills, the personal life of Beverley Chang, the recently appointed head of the Devon and Cornwall police force and his new boss, was still a mystery to him. One got the sense that Chang wanted to keep it that way. Very well. Where Chang lay her hat wasn't LeCarre's business, as long as her hat didn't get in the way of his police work. Time would tell.

'You look beautiful tonight,' LeCarre lovingly told his wife, tenderly.

'You don't look so bad yourself, Detective,' she replied.

When Roger first found Carrie he couldn't believe such a kind, intelligent and hygienic woman could have entered his life. To think, if her sister hadn't been murdered, they'd have never even met. In those early years they often spoke of themselves as blessed (except for the murder of her sister), so lucky to have stumbled upon a perfect companion. They'd made love every night before they went to sleep and every morning after they woke up and then three or four times during the day. Now they were lucky if they made love ten times a week.

They still loved each other, of that there was no doubt. Their marriage, like any other marriage, had had its ups and downs. Carrie felt that LeCarre worked too hard and

43

also, unreasonably, that he didn't contribute enough to the housework. The thing was, Carrie was just much better at cleaning than he was and also had higher standards so always cleaned before LeCarre felt it was needed, so he didn't have a chance. Also, he'd always brought home the proverbial bacon and although she technically earned more money than him and worked longer hours, he was on his feet a lot more so it was more tiring.

Truth be told, Roger was never exactly clear on what Carrie did for a living. He knew it was something to do with computers. Or was it? It was definitely an office job. The thing was, when you had a mind as large and active as Roger LeCarre's it was very hard to concentrate on trivial things like whatever it was that your wife did for a living. Actually, maybe it wasn't in an office, come to think of it. It was just that every day Roger LeCarre dealt with crime scenes, car chases, matters of life and death. What Carrie did, whatever that was, just couldn't compete with Roger's job in terms of its importance.

'What do you do?' Beverley Chang asked Carrie.

'I'm a surgeon.'

LeCarre didn't hear. His attention was drawn to the stage. Rufus Scallion, the city's tubby lord mayor, was approaching the Shure SM58 microphone perched neatly in its stand. It looked like the event that they were all gathered for was about to begin.

'Ladies and gentlemen . . . '

The conversation of seven hundred or so Devonians faded away, their faces now pointed in anticipation towards Exeter's charismatic leader. As always, Scallion wore full ceremonial garb – gold trimmed robes, a giant triangular hat, heavy gold chains around his neck. His face was a near perfect square. On his top lip sat an impressively thick salt-and-pepper moustache. So famous was it that many joked Rufus Scallion must have been born with a moustache. One night a curious Roger LeCarre looked it up to double check and had his suspicions confirmed – it's actually biologically impossible for a baby to be born with a moustache. Scallion's booming voice made the £95 microphone completely unnecessary, another waste of taxpayers' money, thought LeCarre.

'We gather here tonight as we do every year, to celebrate the wonderful city of Exeter and its incredible people. And what a year it's been. A new recycling scheme was successfully rolled out . . . '

'Ha!' LeCarre scornfully exhaled to Jax's amusement.

' . . . new parking bays were introduced on Squire Street and I was proud to be the first lord mayor in our one-thousand-year history to make a TikTok video.'

45

The audience laughed and applauded. Scallion was a politician who knew how to play a crowd. He was like a fat Barack Obama with a West Country accent and a string of drink-driving convictions.

'Soon I'll be coming to the reason why we're all here, the Exeter Person of the Year Award, but first I have an announcement to make. We all know that Exeter is a great city – we feel it in our Exeter bones – but for too long Exeter has been ignored. Some say we live in the shadow of bigger cities like Bristol. *They should be living in the shadow of us!* Did Chris Martin from Coldplay choose to be born in Bristol? No, he did not! Did Beth Gibbons from nineties trip-hop outfit Portishead? Did Toby Buckland, the *main* presenter on BBC2's *Gardeners' World* from 2008 to 2010? No! They did not! They all chose to be born here, in Exeter, because Exeter is the greatest city in the world!'

The crowd cheered enthusiastically. In his mind, LeCarre intelligently drew parallels with the enthusiastic crowds he'd seen in Nazi documentaries, but couldn't help but be swept up in the enthusiasm himself because Rufus Scallion wasn't a Nazi; Nazis are German.

'And soon, ladies and gentlemen, very soon the world will know it because, as you are aware, in less than a week's time we will be the UK Capital of Culture!'

Rapturous applause filled the room.

'The sceptics amongst you, and there will be sceptics, there always are . . . the sceptics will say, "Didn't Exeter only get the UK Capital of Culture because Coventry were finding the costs crippling and pulled out at the last minute?" To those sceptics I say this: we *will* make a success of this because we are Exeter, the birthplace of John Carne Bidwill, the famous nineteenth-century botanist!'

Even louder grew the applause. Scallion's rhetorical skills were incredible.

'When you take a train from London to the West Country, what is the first West Country destination you come to, ladies and gentlemen? Is it Taunton or is it Exeter?'

'Taunton!' shouted the crowd.

'Well, let me ask you this. Is there any reason why it must be Taunton? Did the good Lord Himself ordain from on high that the Great Western Railway service should come to Taunton first and not Exeter?'

'No!' cried the crowd.

'No! You're right, no! What *should* be the first place that you come to?'

'Exeter!'

'Yes! Exeter! EXETER! That is something that we are going to change, my friends. That is something we are going to change, together. And that isn't all we are going to change. When this nation looks west, I don't want them to look to Glastonbury with their filthy festival, to Bristol with their pathetic Clifton Suspension Bridge, to Cornwall with their myriad documentary series about fishing. We want them to look right where they should be looking – to us! To Exeter! To make that happen we need our own landmark, something which simply cannot be ignored, and that is why I am proud to reveal . . . '

Scallion gestured to his right and, suddenly beside him, to the audience's amazement, was a rotating hologram, three times his height.

'The Great Rufus Scallion Exeter Wheel, the biggest Ferris wheel in the whole of Europe. It would be the biggest in the world but they've got one in Dubai which is, well, to be honest, it's just ridiculous. But this, ladies and gentlemen, will put our city on the map. The whole world will know about Exeter now! Construction begins tomorrow morning and I'm delighted to say that the first people to ride the wheel will do so this Friday evening at the celebrations for our first night as UK Capital of Culture. This is our moment, Exeter! This is our time!'

The whole room rose to its feet, Detective Roger LeCarre included. He crashed his giant hands together, like a head-on collision between two trucks but one in which the trucks reversed and then kept doing the same thing, which is to say he clapped. Were he not so masculine, tears may have streamed down his face.

'And now,' said Scallion, 'I come to the climax of the evening.'

LeCarre looked at his watch. Come to think of it, it was a little odd that the whole event had only lasted around ten minutes. That was only around a sixth of the time he'd spent inside Melanie Fade that day.

'The Exeter Person of the Year Award. I have just taken a moment to talk about the bright future this city has ahead of it. That future can only be secure if our citizens feel safe . . . '

LeCarre stared into the middle distance, deep in intelligent thought. He had never seen himself as a parochial Exeter loyalist; he was a man of the world, born in Totnes. He enjoyed cuisine from the likes of India, China and Italy. He didn't care where you came from – whether it was Exeter or Exmouth, Bodmin or Bude – but here was a man giving the beaten-down people of the city something to believe in. Just the other day, the University of Exeter had dropped from ninth to twelfth place in the national university league tables. A city couldn't take that kind of humiliation – not

49

for long, anyway – but here was this great man offering them hope.

Charlie Fade would never ride the Great Rufus Scallion Exeter Wheel. He had already taken his final trip – the one to the ever after. LeCarre felt inspired to make sure that other young men and women, caught up in the gang violence that plagued the city with a tsunami of crime, would survive to see the wheel, to ride it and to help Exeter become the city it could be.

'... Ladies and gentlemen, it gives me great pleasure to announce that tonight's Exeter Person of the Year is ... DETECTIVE ROGER LECARRE.'

# SIX

The award had come as a complete shock. You didn't get into policing for the trophies. Sure, they came with the territory, but that's not why you got into it. You became a police officer to protect your community from crime, and also for the salary. Without the salary, you could in theory still work full time catching criminals, but in order to pay your bills you may find yourself committing crime, thus creating a vicious circle, a world in which all criminals and all police officers were essentially the same people, catching each other – and that wouldn't be good for anyone.

Luckily we didn't live in such a world. We lived in a world where Detective Roger LeCarre and all his friends from the force were celebrating his win at the Crown and Goose pub. He was standing at the bar with DI Todd Gatting and DI Rico Hernandez, shooting the proverbial shit, Gatting's and Hernandez's wives rolling their proverbial eyes. Jax and LeCarre's wife, Carrie, were sitting down together, chuckling heartily. One big family. Exeter could be a dark place, but not tonight, not here in the Crown and Goose, and that wasn't just because of the uncomfortably fluorescent lighting.

If the world outside those pub doors was their hell, then here inside the Crown and Goose was their salvation. A place where men could be men and where women could be women, within reason. This was a pub as a pub should be – three lagers on tap, a 3.8 per cent, a 4.2 per cent and a foreign 5 per cent. Guinness, cider and four cask ales, two of them rotating guest ales, two of them local stalwarts, but nothing weird like chocolate porter. LeCarre was supposed to be on the wagon, but it was difficult to stay on the wagon when the wagon was still moving. From marking the anniversary of your partner's death, to passing your MOT, to celebrating winning Exeter Person of the Year – there was always a reason to drink.

LeCarre still felt a glow from being in the presence of Rufus Scallion. For a brief moment Roger could appreciate what it must have been like to meet Nelson Mandela or Nick Clegg. Was it all a front? Scallion's passion for Exeter certainly came across as authentic. The giant Ferris wheel seemed ambitious. The city was bankrupt. Where was the money coming from? I suppose if everyone in Exeter paid an extra pound in council tax or something then that would probably make an extra billion pounds or something. LeCarre didn't have time to do the exact sums but that wasn't his job: his job was stopping crime, and judging by the size of the trophy sat on the bar beside him, he was pretty good at it.

LeCarre was too modest to admit it but the award was well deserved. He was like a modern-day St Patrick, but instead of driving all the snakes from Ireland, he'd driven all the triads from Devon and Cornwall.

'And don't come back!' he'd shouted, last year, when the last triad crossed the Devon border and headed to Dorset. It was an impressive feat but in LeCarre's eyes, just a drop in the ocean. He hadn't gotten rid of crime, he'd just gotten rid of Chinese crime and that wasn't enough.

'Another Ruddles, lads?' said Hernandez.

'Is it a lunar eclipse?' said Gatting.

'Must be if he's buying a round,' said LeCarre.

The banter between them went at such a slick pace, one could be forgiven for thinking they were a high-quality sketch trio with a primetime show on Radio 4.

LeCarre took a sip of the Suffolk-brewed guest ale with

hoppy, citrus undertones and studied his comrades, fondly: Hernandez – the Mexican hothead, never did paperwork because he was completely illiterate, but knew how to get a conviction; Gatting – the longest-serving officer on the force, a legend, a gentle giant, 19 stone but almost all of it heart. And then LeBron Jax. LeCarre looked over to him; his arms were around Carrie's body, kindly showing her how to hold a pool cue. If Gatting and Hernandez were LeCarre's brothers then Jax was something closer – a conjoined twin?

The world may be grim but LeCarre was on top of it. Who killed Charlie Fade? Would Exeter make a success of the UK Capital of Culture? Would he live to see a world without crime? He didn't know. Through the alcohol haze he could only be sure of one thing – the lads from the Devon and Cornwall police force were his family and none of them would ever let him down.


Detective Roger LeCarre arrived home to find his wife in bed with LeBron Jax. Apparently they'd been having an affair for six months. Perhaps LeCarre should have seen the signs. Jax and Carrie had always seemed to get along rather well but Roger had thought that was a good thing – they were one big family. It had struck him as a little odd when Jax and Carrie went on a two-week barge holiday together in the Norfolk Broads but he supposed that maybe they were planning a surprise birthday party for him or something. He didn't want to come across as paranoid.

He'd been having such a good time with Hernandez and Gatting at the bar in the Crown and Goose – telling stories of old arrests, arm wrestling, debating the latest Booker Prize shortlist – that when Jax offered to take Carrie home he'd thanked him for being a good friend.

'You're a good friend, Jax,' he'd said.

If only he could go back in time and say those words sarcastically, but time travel hadn't been invented yet and if you thought about it, it never would be, because if it had been then we would already have been visited by time travellers from the future – do you see what I'm getting at?

LeCarre had a penthouse apartment in the centre of town, just above a Paddy Power, opposite a Superdrug. When he was working on a case he would often sleep there. LeCarre in the depths of his work could be a difficult man to be around so the understanding between he and Carrie was that it was better for her and their daughter if Roger sometimes had his own space. Also, it was a good place to do his jigsaw puzzles because Carrie complained that they took up the kitchen table at home and affected dinner time.

That night, at the Crown and Goose, LeCarre had told

Carrie he'd stay at the penthouse. He was going to see the pathologist for a report on Charlie Fade's body in the morning and wanted to get into the right frame of mind. It was a last-minute decision to go home instead. He'd remembered he hadn't renewed his TV licence at the penthouse, and not wanting to commit a crime by watching live TV but also wanting to catch the end of *Match of the Day 2*, he decided to take a taxi to the fully TV-licensed family home.

There he heard it – the unmistakable sound of another man penetrating his wife. Thinking his ears must be playing tricks on him, he opened the bedroom door, his bedroom door, to discover his partner on top of his partner.

'Roger! I can explain!' said his wife, still in the reverse cowgirl position Roger had read about in books.

'Be my guest! Come on! Explain! Look at me and explain why you're sat on top of my partner's penis with my old police hat on your head. I'm all ears, Carrie. I am literally just a pile of ears.'

But she couldn't explain. She couldn't say a damn thing. LeCarre looked at LeBron Jax, his supposed brother.

'Get out of my house.'

It was like a scene from a really good film.

Jax walked out into the Exeter night like a terrorist who'd just set a bomb on a marriage.

A hoot from above. An owl in a tree, looking down on LeBron Jax. Being a bird, the owl could not comprehend what it was looking at, but if it could just for a moment transcend its avian world, it would be disgusted. Betrayal – the famous noun had taken human form. Five of LeCarre's partners had died. In his eyes, Jax was now number six. *It was this death that hurt the most.*

# SEVEN

The water shimmered in the morning sunlight like a Kia Ceed fresh from the showroom. Detective Roger LeCarre picked up another stone and skimmed it across the River Exe, Exeter's centrepiece and in his opinion one of Britain's top three most under-appreciated bodies of water. Here, by the Trews Weir Suspension Bridge, in a tranquil patch of rocks, not far from Halfords and Majestic Wine, was where LeCarre came to reflect on life.

In his leather jacket and brown brogue boots you could be forgiven for thinking he was some kind of male model advertising a vitamin supplement, but LeCarre was nothing of the sort – he was a copper who hadn't slept. He reached into his inside pocket and took another sip of White Russian from his stainless-steel hip flask. The cream was beginning to curdle. Just like his soul.

'Trust!' he vocalised, letting the word elongate dramatically in his mouth. 'Truuuuuuuuuuuust!'

It took eight or nine seconds to say it, longer than it had taken for his marriage to fall apart. How could Carrie do that to him? Yes, LeCarre had been unfaithful and, yes, he'd been irritating Carrie lately by turning the living room into his own personal dojo to practise his capoeira and, yes, he'd recently suggested they have an open relationship, but there are lines *you do not cross*.

He threw another stone into the water and watched it leap seventeen times, one leap for every year he'd been with Carrie. One leap for every Body Shop bath bomb he'd got her for Christmas, one leap for every Valentine's Day bunch of luxury flowers from Esso. How could she?

*How could she?*

LeCarre looked at the ground around him. How many stones? There were probably enough to keep skimming for another four or five months. He couldn't do that, though, much as he'd like to. There was a murderer to catch. It was nearly twenty-four hours since he'd been to the crime scene and all LeCarre had done was have sex with the victim's mother, witness the end of his marriage and win Exeter Person of the Year. Time to get to work. But first, he had a score to settle.

# EIGHT

*Crash!*

LeBron Jax's naked body slammed against the wall of lockers in the Central Exeter Police Station changing room.

'Nice shower? Did you wash the scum from your soul or just my wife's sweat?'

'Rog . . . '

'Don't call me Rog. Only my wife calls me Rog and I gotta tell you, Jax, that privilege is currently under review.'

*Crash!*

Jax's body making contact with the lockers again.

'Roger, you've every right to be angry. There's a lot you don't know . . . '

'A lot I don't know, huh? You're fucking my wife *and* you're throwing me off The Enforcers.' The Enforcers was their pub quiz team. 'I gotta tell you, Jax. I don't like

60

where this friendship is headed. I'll tell you something I *do* know. That Riga is the capital of Latvia and not Lithuania, something that you insisted two weeks ago, thus losing us the quiz.'

*Crash!*

This time it was LeCarre's body slamming against the lockers.

'You know damn well I said I wasn't a hundred per cent sure,' said Jax. 'At least I don't keep getting my Brontës mixed up.'

*Crash!*

Now the two bodies were slamming into each other. It was like the break-up of Yugoslavia. Tensions which had been kept bottled up were now in the open and all-out war had broken out.

*Crash!*

This time it was both men's bodies hitting the lockers, courtesy of the giant ham-like hands of Detective Todd Gatting.

'Break it up, lads. The enemy is out there, not in here.'

Gatting's booming voice reverberated around the room like a jumbo jet revving up inside a hangar.

'You could have fooled me,' spat LeCarre.

The changing-room door opened. Now the changing

room filled with the sound of 6-inch heels touching the ground – Chief Superintendent Beverley Chang.

'In my office, LeCarre. Now!'

LeCarre strolled in like the cat who got the cream and also was the cream, the cream of the Devon and Cornwall police force, but this cream had gone bad. Chang had cream on her mind.

'Ma'am. I'm sorry. I can explain.'

'Scones,' said Chang.

'I beg your pardon, ma'am?'

'Scones, LeCarre. Scones!'

Was this a clever diversion tactic, to take LeCarre's mind off his rage at LeBron? If so, it was working.

'Both you and I know I'm not from round these parts,' Chang continued. 'I'm from London, but I'm the new head of the Devon and Cornwall police force and I can't be seen to be getting it wrong, but one guy from Devon tells me it's cream on first and one guy from Cornwall tells me it's jam on first. What's the deal, LeCarre?'

'Ah, the scone question. Or should I say scone? The whole thing's a fucking minefield. The answer's simple, ma'am, but you're not gonna like it. You're going to have to stay away from them altogether. It's just too risky. One slip-up, you seen in a Penzance café eating a scone Devon-style? I'm not burying another copper, ma'am.'

Chang could hear the pain in his eyes. She was an experienced police officer from the Met and she'd just won LeCarre's respect. Chang knew what too few coppers knew: the way to calm an enraged man was to ask his advice on something. LeCarre felt emasculated by Jax's adventures with Carrie but here was an attractive older woman allowing LeCarre to penetrate her where it really mattered – *her mind.*

'Look, LeCarre, I don't know what's going on between you and Jax . . .'

'It's really—'

*'And I don't want to know.* The important thing is that it doesn't affect your work. This city needs cleaning up, preferably in time for the Capital of Culture celebrations, and I need my best copper to have his mind on the job. Is your mind on the job, LeCarre?'

'Ma'am. I want you to know that—'

'Is your mind on the job, LeCarre?'

'Yes, ma'am.'

'Good. Now it's clear to me that you and Jax can't work together, not now. Maybe you'll one day work together again like Robbie Williams and his writing partner Guy

Chambers did after many years of working apart, but this city can't wait for you two to sort your shit out.'

'Understood. For the record, ma'am, I'd just like to say that the song "Angels", which Williams and Chambers wrote together, is the greatest song this country has ever produced,' said LeCarre.

'I'm glad you feel the same. Now, I don't know how you get the results you do, LeCarre, but the eyes of the world are on us and I need to make sure you're doing things by the book,' said Chang.

The Book. Detective Roger LeCarre was tired of hearing about The Book. He liked books, sure – he'd read more than 100,000, mainly biographies of Hitler – but The Book was not to his liking.

'Maybe my habit of getting results has something to do with my dislike for The Book ma'am,' said LeCarre.

'I thought as much.' Chang looked down at the paper on her desk. 'I see you had an incident with a taser going off in an interview room last month.'

'What can I say? I'm no good with modern technology.'

Chang read further. 'You visited a school last week and broke an eight-year-old boy's arm.'

'He was talking back and . . . '

'And? And what, LeCarre? You broke his arm?'

'I felt my life was in danger, ma'am.'

'There have been accusations of planting evidence,' said Chang.

'What can I say? I'm a keen gardener.'

'Planting evidence is a crime, LeCarre,' said Chang.

'No it's not – crime is a crime. The simple truth is there are currently eight hundred and twenty-seven people sitting in prison, thanks to me.'

LeCarre always kept a running total of this figure. By his calculations he could take personal credit for nearly 1 per cent of the country's prison population. Just a fortnight ago, when he and Carrie had returned from their Friday-night Zizzi's, he realised the babysitter had eaten one of their yogurts. Within an hour Cindy was charged and awaiting trial. Some might say LeCarre was harsh, but the way he saw things, if you're capable of stealing a peach melba yogurt, which he had been looking forward to eating before bed, then you're capable of murdering a child. The streets were safer with Cindy off them. A criminal is a criminal. Zero tolerance. But it seemed Chief Superintendent Beverley Chang had zero tolerance of *his* methods.

Chang was an attractive woman of a certain age, specifically fifty-four. Thick black hair emanated from her scalp and let gravity do its work, dragging it beautifully downwards past her shoulders. Her lips were a striking bright red, which LeCarre assumed was the result of lipstick rather than some kind of weird condition. Her elegant perfume hung in the air like a pleasant gas. She took one of her long, experienced fingers and pressed the intercom on the landline phone.

'Rhodes, I'd like you to come in now, please.'

A young man of no more than twenty-three entered the room so gingerly you could have peeled him, grated him and stuck him in a curry. He looked like the academic type – glasses, tweed jacket, a leather briefcase. His tiny arms hung from his pathetic body like two pieces of string. This guy's so weedy, I should be impounding him as evidence, thought LeCarre to himself in a clever joke around the word 'weed', which is the street name for cannabis.

'Take a seat, Tim. Roger, I'd like you to meet Detective Tim Rhodes. Tim recently graduated from Leicester De Montfort University with a first-class degree in criminology.'

'You've got to be joking,' disdained LeCarre.

'You'll have to excuse Detective LeCarre, Tim. He's a little rough around the edges. I'm hoping you might be able to smooth those edges out for us.'

'Ma'am.' LeCarre was becoming animated now, like a character from a film made by Pixar or DreamWorks or

Aardman Animations or a TV show on CBeebies or something. 'This isn't a university and this sure as heck isn't a library. This is the Devon and Cornwall police force. Tim, I'm sure you're a lovely guy but you don't become a detective by going to university.'

Tim wriggled uncomfortably in his chair.

'The world is changing, LeCarre,' said Chang. 'It's time you changed with it. Tim has spent four years studying policing techniques. He's a very capable detective; I think you could learn a lot from him. Tim, why don't you tell Roger about your thesis?'

Tim cleared his throat and touched his spectacles – two classic geek moves, noted LeCarre.

'Well, um, my thesis . . . well, I wanted to discover why crime had reduced in Flemish communities in the late 1990s at the same time as a reduction in street policing – what we might colloquially call "bobbies on the beat". My studies were able to determine that greater community engagement, such as government-funded cookery courses and theatre workshops with young offenders, as well as a greater emphasis on predicting where crimes might occur through algorithmic methodology, were remarkably effective.'

LeCarre stared straight ahead. Was this what police work was coming to? Were handcuffs and truncheons about to be replaced with a packet of firm tofu and a copy of *New Statesman*? There was a place for people like Tim Rhodes but it wasn't here – it was an organic farmers' market. Were there only three choices now? You can have a partner who dies, a partner who sexes your wife or a partner who's probably fifteen minutes away from offering you a slice of his homemade goddamn sourdough?

'Let me ask you a question, Detective Tim Rhodes. You went to university, I'm sure you're no stranger to questions. So here's my question: have you ever broken down the door of a St Austell crack den only to be met by a seven-foot bastard with meat cleaver in one hand and a box of fireworks in the other? Have you ever had to choose between saving a group of schoolchildren and saving Exeter's oldest tree? And then had to live with that choice for the rest of your life? Have you ever had to tell a man that his wife has been murdered and then realised that you had the wrong house and had to do it all over again and then realised that you had the wrong house again and then had to recheck the address and then do it all over again? Well, have you? Have you? Have you, Tim Rhodes? Have you? Have you? Answer me, Tim Rhodes! Have you?'

By the sheer power of his voice, Roger LeCarre had

Tim Rhodes pinned against the wall of Beverley Chang's glass office.

'All right, LeCarre, that's enough,' said Chang 'You've made your point.'

Chang threw a copy of *The Times* on to the desk in front of her. 'We're front-page news. *National* front-page news.' LeCarre's blue eyes directed themselves away from Tim Rhodes and towards the newspaper.

## MURDER IN CENTRAL EXETER: POLICE HAVE NO LEADS

'Is that true, LeCarre?' asked Chang, pointedly. 'We have no leads?'

'Nothing concrete, ma'am. I have some theories.'

'This is not your average murder, Roger. The body was found right in the centre of Exeter. Right outside St Pancras Church, just yards from our blessed cathedral. That doesn't reflect well on this city. I don't care if you're Exeter's Person of the Year, I don't care if your private life is a mess – heck, LeCarre, isn't everybody's? The simple fact is I need you to find out who killed Charlie Fade before the largest Ferris wheel in Europe is revealed this Friday night at the UK Capital of Culture celebrations in the centre of Exeter, which coincidentally is where Charlie Fade's body was found. Am I making myself clear?' Chang banged her fist against the desk, sexily.

'Yes, ma'am,' said LeCarre.

'Excellent. You're going to see the pathologist now, is that right?' said Chang.

'Yes, ma'am.'

'Good. Take Rhodes with you. He's a smart young man, LeCarre. Use him. You never know, you might actually find him to be rather helpful.'

'No offence, but I think I'll go on my own. If I need any nineteenth-century French poetry translated, Tim, I'll let you know,' said LeCarre.

'*Take him, LeCarre.*'

'Ma'am, I really don't—'

'It's an order.'

'An order? Why?'

'*Because Tim Rhodes is your new partner.*'

# NINE

A million droplets of rain fell from the sky and landed on the Exeter ground, which if you think about it for a moment isn't actually that much rain really, just a shower. The all-weather tyres of Detective Roger LeCarre's Kia Ceed came to a comfortable standstill at a set of traffic lights. A little girl in a yellow raincoat and wellies crossed the road in front of him, playfully splashing in the puddles. Could she be Charlie Fade's murderer? Seemed unlikely, but if Jax and Carrie could betray him like they had then anything was possible. Perhaps he should haul the girl in for questioning now, see if she confessed.

His mind was all over the place. Not only did he have to solve Charlie Fade's murder, not only was his life falling apart, not only had he just been lumped with a new, pathetic-looking wimp of a partner, but he still had to sort out his energy provider before the new tariff kicked in.

The light went green and LeCarre accelerated, comfortably speeding away from a 2011 Peugeot 506.

'Nice car,' said Rhodes, making his third attempt at small talk.

'Thank you. It is. What do you drive, Professor? A VW camper van, no doubt.'

'I actually get around on a bike. Better for the environment, you know,' said Rhodes.

'The environment, huh? Let me ask you this: if climate change is happening then how come it's raining? Answer me that, Professor,' said LeCarre, proving to Rhodes that you didn't need a university degree to make a well-thought-out and intelligent point.

Silence.

If only the rain could wash away the sins of the city. A nice thought, but anyone with patio furniture knows that rain just makes things dirtier – as dirty as a marriage, as dirty as murder.

'Seeing as we're going to be working together, you might as well bring me up to speed on the case,' said Rhodes.

'Surely you know who the killer is already? You mean to tell me they didn't tell you who killed Charlie Fade at your poxy university? I want my taxes back.' LeCarre's hangover wasn't impeding his ability to shred someone to pieces with pure intellect. It was, perhaps, impeding his manners.

'There're a lot of things they didn't teach me, Detective,' said Rhodes. 'Things I'm hoping I can learn from you. I know you may have some preconceived ideas about my ability as a copper, coming from university and everything, but I want you to know that I've taken some time to study your career and admire you very much. If I can become half the copper you are, I'll have done well.'

LeCarre turned to look at Rhodes. 'All right, lesson number one: ditch the bow tie.'

Rhodes blushed with embarrassment as LeCarre continued his lesson.

'A bow tie might fit in in a lecture hall or a student union or a string quartet or whatever it is you're used to, Detective. I'm sure you all wear bow ties at university, but it won't fit in out here, on the streets. Right now, if I'm a criminal, I look at you and I see fresh meat, ripe for the grinder.'

'OK. Noted,' said the humbled Rhodes.

'And what's that on your finger, Detective Rhodes? That a wedding ring? Don't tell me it's a wedding ring. Tell me it's a wedding ring and I am getting up to ninety miles per hour and driving us straight into a wall. I'll do it, Rhodes.

I've done it before and I'll do it again. Is that a wedding ring? Don't lie to me, Rhodes. Is that a wedding ring?' Bullying was an important part of working with younger officers and LeCarre was one of the best at it.

'Yes ... it's a wedding ring,' said Rhodes, meekly.

'Get out!' LeCarre leaned over Rhodes and opened his passenger door. 'Get out now. I'm not slowing down, I've got a pathologist to see. Get out of this car now and take that bloody wedding ring with you.'

Rhodes slammed the door shut and attempted to defend himself.

'*You're* wearing a wedding ring.'

'Am I?' LeCarre looked down at his wedding ring, took it off and threw it out of his driver's side window. 'No, I'm not. A wedding ring signals a weakness, tells the world that there's someone you love. I don't love anyone, Rhodes, and I sure as crap hope you don't either.'

'I love my wife, yes. I don't think that's a weakness and I don't think it's going to affect my work. She supports me,' said Rhodes.

'You sure about that, Detective? You sure she's not sprawled out on a desk right now, steaming up some professor's glasses?' said LeCarre.

'Yes, I'm sure. She loves me.'

'Well, in that case she won't mind if you take that wedding ring off your finger and throw it out of the window.'

Both men were silent for a moment, until LeCarre spoke up again.

'I can hear that big brain of yours whirring away, Detective, trying to calculate if I'm serious or not. I'm deadly serious, Rhodes. Throw that ring out of the window right now or I am driving us straight back to the station and telling Chang that Detective Rhodes can't come to work today because he's just pissed his pants,' said LeCarre.

'But . . . ' Rhodes thought for a moment. 'I mean, she'll be able to see that I didn't piss my pants.'

'I'll piss on them for you, buddy. I've done it before and I'll do it again. Throw your wedding ring out of the window now or I am turning this car around, taking you back to the police station, pissing on your pants and then taking you to Chang and telling her that you pissed your own pants. It's a very simple choice, my friend.'

Rhodes looked down at the gold band on his finger. He and Pippa had picked it out together. They'd spent all their savings to buy the rings. They didn't need money, all they needed was each other. Now Rhodes had got himself a job with the Devon and Cornwall police force and dragged Pippa to Exeter to start his career. She'd had to give up a place on the Team GB Olympic Equestrian Team but she'd insisted on supporting Tim and his dreams. His success could be her success. She didn't care about the five Olympic rings, she only cared about the rings on their fingers, the rings that signified their love for one another.

His clammy hands serving as a lubricant, Rhodes shimmied the ring off his finger and threw it out of the window of LeCarre's moving car. He watched it bounce down the road behind him through the passenger wing mirror.

'So you want to be a real police officer, huh?' said LeCarre, respectfully.

'Yes, sir, yes, sir I do.'

'Good. Then let's go look at a dead body.'


The body lay on the slab as if it was dead because it was and this was a morgue. Detective Roger LeCarre and the attractive British Indian forensic Gita Patel inspected it grimly. Some of the lads on the force thought a woman shouldn't be in such a ghoulish job. LeCarre didn't have a problem with it. As far as he was concerned, a woman could do any job she liked except for pub quizmaster because women did too many questions about soaps and, in his experience, were a little tardy timewise and had poor microphone technique.

'We have to stop meeting like this, Charlie, people will get ideas,' joked LeCarre.

Charlie didn't laugh because Charlie was dead. Gallows humour was how cops like LeCarre and pathologists like Patel got through the endless parade of misery. Detective Tim Rhodes, who stood more tentatively, a couple of metres from the corpse, wasn't yet ready to join in.

Patel grabbed Charlie Fade's jaw, moved it up and down and did a silly voice.

'Come on, Detective Rhodes! Give us a kiss!'

'You'll have to excuse Detective Rhodes, Gita,' said LeCarre. 'This is his first visit to a morgue.'

From the look on Tim Rhodes's green face, if he had his way, it would be his last.

'All right, Gita, give us the lowdown,' said LeCarre, casually leaning on a different cadaver on another slab. He felt at home in a morgue, more at home than he had ever felt in any house, certainly his own considering recent developments. Perhaps he should sleep here tonight, next to the victims of crime, people who actually needed him rather than his wife who clearly didn't.

'I've analysed the body using science and I'm able to say

confidently that Charlie Fade died on Saturday night, sometime between ten thirty p.m. and ten thirty-five p.m. Sorry,
I can't be more specific.'

Rhodes made a note in his notepad, LeCarre in his
giant mind.

Patel continued her dark presentation.

'At the time of death, Charlie Fade had eleven different
herbs and spices in his system. We're working under the
assumption he had a KFC for dinner.'

'That would account for the grease on his fingers,'
said Rhodes.

'Very good, Detective,' said Patel. 'But there was something else, some kind of stimulant.'

'Honey mustard?' said LeCarre.

'No. It looks to be some kind of new drug. We've seen it
in a few of our cases in the last few months.'

'Gasmask,' said LeCarre, emphatically.

'Gasmask?' Patel tilted her head, betraying her arousal at
LeCarre's knowledge.

'That's what they're calling it on the streets. As addictive
as heroin, as available as Cadbury's chocolate buttons.'

'How does it make you feel?' asked Rhodes.

LeCarre's eyes shot at Rhodes like lasers from two snipers
sitting side by side.

'I don't intend on finding out, Rhodes. Do you? First I heard of it was some kid in Plymouth, broke into the Sealife Centre and said he wanted to fight a shark. Spent a night in the cells, woke up the next day and blamed it on Gasmask. Right now, we don't know where it's coming from – we just know that it's sending the kids of Devon and Cornwall wild.'

LeCarre was never more passionate than when talking about the negative effects of drugs or why Dyson vacuum cleaners are incredibly overrated. He felt that drugs left a trail of destruction wherever they went and that the Dyson's pleasing design masked inferior suction and reliability when compared with leading competitors.

This Gasmask was a real problem. Something about it seemed to be attracting youngsters from respectable homes. Perhaps it was its newness. Kids always wanted the latest thing – the hot new trainers, the latest Jonathan Franzen novel – but unfortunately this year the 'latest thing' was a killer drug. How it made the taker feel, LeCarre could never truly know – they were too mashed up to describe it themselves – but it seemed to make them want to move. The week before he was interrogating a suspect who suddenly started dancing as soon as LeCarre's phone rang. But this drug was no disco.

'Could that have been what killed him? The Gasmask?' asked Rhodes.

'No. Charlie Fade died from trauma caused by a massive loss of blood thanks to this stab wound.' Gita Patel dramatically pulled back the sheet that had been covering the bottom two thirds of Fade's body like a magician revealing the results of a trick which had gone very wrong.

This was a stab wound unlike any LeCarre had ever seen before. Rhodes vomited on to the floor immediately, only able to let out a meek 'Ugh-du' by way of apology. LeCarre and Patel rolled their four eyes in unison.

'Samurai sword?' asked LeCarre, fearing the triads had returned with Japanese weaponry.

'I shouldn't think so,' said Patel. 'This looks to me like something bigger. Clearly some kind of bladed weapon was used, but, I have to say, it's rather unusual.'

'Chainsaw?' asked LeCarre, while Rhodes mopped up his own vomit and tried not to vomit again.

'It's possible,' said Patel, moving her hand towards her chin in scientific thought. 'But this wound is a result of one direct entry into the belly, one direct thrust. In my experience, most chainsaw deaths involve the weapon being moved around inside the victim while the murderer maniacally laughs.'

LeCarre nodded. Patel was as sharp as the weapon used to murder Charlie Fade. Whatever that was.

'There's something else,' said Patel, pointing towards Fade's chest.

So shocking was the wound, LeCarre hadn't noticed the two words carved into Charlie Fade's skin. He leaned in: SEMPER FIDELIS.

'This looks fresh. My analysis shows it was probably carved into his skin at around ten thirty-six p.m., immediately after he was murdered,' said Patel.

Rhodes then braced himself and viewed the words.

'*Semper fidelis*, it's Latin,' he said.

'Pah!' LeCarre exhaled. 'Latin. I suppose that's your first language, is it, Rhodes? I suppose you all talk Latin to each other in your university poetry slams and your university croquet tournaments. Well, come on then, what does it mean?'

'*Semper fidelis*. I can't remember. *But I can find out.*'

# TEN

'Just give me a second. I'm trying to get some reception.'
Rhodes was looking at his 64GB iPhone Pro as they walked
through the morgue car park. Rain had made way for
the sun but, unlike Devon's second-largest city, Detective
Roger LeCarre's mood hadn't brightened.

'Put it away, Rhodes. You don't solve murders on phones,
you solve them on the streets,' husked LeCarre.

'It'll just take me a second. We might as well find out
what it means.'

'It doesn't mean anything,' said LeCarre. 'It's Latin!
How do you think we solved murders before smart-
phones, Rhodes? You think we all walked around with an
*Encyclopaedia Britannica*? You think we waited to see what
Latin phrase the killer had written on the body and then
pulled out our Latin dictionaries?'

'Seriously, sir. I've got 4G, I'm just putting it into Google Translate. I'll have an answer in literally ten seconds.' Rhodes was standing still besides LeCarre's car now.

LeCarre swung his leg-of-lamb-like arm and batted the phone out of Rhodes's hand. Roger leaned into Rhodes's face, close enough so that Rhodes would be able to smell the Trebor Extra Strong mints on his breath. 'If we're going to work together, we're going to do it –' LeCarre leaned in three inches closer '– *my way.*'

'Yes, boss. Your way.'

'Good. Now get in the car.'

Rhodes picked up his phone, undamaged thanks to a quality protective case, and did as LeCarre said.

LeCarre stepped on the gas, which is American for accelerator. They passed Exeter University and, just minutes later, HM Prison Exeter. Both were in the centre of town and stood like differing beacons showing the citizens two vastly different destinations. If Tim Rhodes was a man of the university path and Donkey Malone was a man of the criminal, then LeCarre was a man of neither. Instead he sat in the middle, able to converse with prince and pauper, criminal and scholar. He was an everyman, a bit like Bradley Walsh.

LeCarre parked outside Exeter CCTV Headquarters,

using Kia Smart Park Assist, and turned to Rhodes. 'See if you can get any footage at the crime scene and surrounding area on Saturday night. Find out who was there, heck, you might even see the murder. Be careful not to vomit again, Rhodes, you might get yourself a reputation.'

'Where are you going?' asked Rhodes.

'Where am I going? I'm going to the ghetto.'

Across the river. Westside. Eastside had its problems, sure, but it also had the cathedral, the cobbled streets, the history, the Bill Douglas Cinema Museum. It had hope. Westside didn't have hope. Just a TK Maxx, a few rough pubs and a lower life expectancy. Time moved more slowly here. It was like the people were walking through treacle. The air seemed thicker, although in actuality that was unlikely because air is air.

LeCarre was still feeling the night before. The drink, the lack of sleep, the end of his marriage. He wasn't operating at optimum LeCarre and he needed to be. He parked his car and stepped into a corner shop. Sugar could help.

Perusing the refrigerator, Detective Roger LeCarre saw the usual: Coca-Cola, Tango, 7up, Tizer, some of the finest carbonated drinks known to man. But what troubled him was something else resting in that chilled chamber – crime.

LeCarre picked up the can of Diet Coke – he wanted to be sure – but there it was in black and white, or grey and red to be precise: NOT TO BE SOLD SEPARATELY.

The detective turned to eye the shopkeeper and assess the room for danger. This was no longer a harmless corner shop, it was an epicentre of crime. There are fifty-seven pressure points on a human body, all of which when pressed correctly can cause excruciating pain. Between his hands and his feet, LeCarre had seventeen digits. Over the years, he'd lost two fingers and a toe in various incidents out on the beat – part of the job. LeCarre hurdled the counter and sank his remaining digits into seventeen different pressure points on the shopkeeper.

'I bet you thought you'd get away with it, didn't ya? *Didn't* ya?'

'Arghhhh!' cried the retailer, in agony.

LeCarre held him suspended in the air while he awaited backup. When PC Philippa Swann finally arrived, LeCarre hurled the shopkeeper into the back of the cop car like a bag of freshly cut potatoes into a chip pan.

'I suppose you thought it was a victimless crime. Tell that to the CEO of the Coca-Cola company, you evil bastard,' LeCarre said as he shut the door and gave Swann a nod which said take this retailer back to the police station and charge him. He'd only been in the ghetto for five minutes, all he'd done was nip into a shop for a drink and a KitKat Chunky, and he'd already made an arrest. LeCarre was like an industrial-strength vacuum cleaner, hoovering up criminals. But the man he'd come to see might be a little harder to suck – Donkey Malone.

Anyone west of Yeovil with a passing interest in the underworld knew Donkey Malone. The Skibblemead Estate was Donkey's domain, the base from which he operated his far-reaching empire.

A lad of no more than fourteen was leaning against a lamp post, chewing Wrigley's spearmint gum. LeCarre took a ten-pound note from his pocket and tore it in two. He handed one piece to the befuddled kid.

'Watch my Kia Ceed for me and you get the other half.'

'Sure. I'll watch it for ya,' squeaked the boy.

'Good. Work hard in school, kid, and maybe one day you'll be driving a car with a DAB radio, USB, Bluetooth connectivity and a reversing camera fitted as standard.'

Some on the force would have thought that just by stepping into the estate LeCarre was putting his life in danger. As a tax-paying citizen, with a respect for the law and a fully operational Nectar card, he was entering enemy territory. He was outside the Green Zone now. Cars with their road tax expired, loft conversions that clearly didn't meet Exeter City Council planning guidelines – everywhere you looked was crime.

Three schoolgirls of eleven or so started to skip. Was that some kind of code? Was this a signal that the po-po were on the block and it was time for Donkey to move his stash? Or were they just inspired by the government's This Girl Can initiative to encourage activity amongst girls? It was hard to tell. Luckily, LeCarre was fluent in West Country patois and was able to communicate without arousing suspicion.

'All right, my lovers? Where's Donkey at then?' he said, casually leaning against a postbox to show that he was comfortable in his surroundings while keeping one hand on his taser, just in case one of the girls kicked off.

The tallest of the three pointed towards the estate's towering tower block, the four-storey Benson Building. So, Donkey was in his lair. Such was his success as a criminal that he could no doubt live wherever he liked, but Donkey sought sanctuary amongst his people – the underclass. The local library's photocopier was broken, the Chinese takeaway had a three-star hygiene rating, the school's recent Ofsted report had said 'needs improvement'; this was not a desirable place to live but it was where Donkey Malone gave his orders and it was where Donkey Malone lay his heathen head.

So why wasn't Donkey behind bars? If the whole world

knew he was a villain, why wasn't he detained at Her Majesty's pleasure? A bastard like Malone should be giving Her Majesty pleasure day and night, right? But Donkey was too clever. He never got his hands dirty and, if he did, he always scrubbed them clean before any copper had a chance to look at them. The dealing, the stealing, the murdering, the recording of podcasts which broke strict copyright infringement rules – that was all done by Donkey's foot soldiers, kids like Charlie Fade.

As LeCarre walked up the stairwell of the Benson Building, the beat grew louder – he felt like a nineteenth-century explorer approaching a tribe, except this time the drums were coming from the radio in Donkey's flat blaring Kiss FM.

LeCarre arrived at Donkey's door and steeled himself. This wasn't their first encounter. They'd met many times before, like Federer and Nadal, two legends of the game. If LeCarre was Federer then today's match would be on clay, Nadal's surface. But they wouldn't be playing tennis, they'd be having a good old match of good against evil. Sticking with the tennis analogy for a moment, the ultimate goal was to hope LeCarre's one-handed backhand could ask enough questions of Malone's ground strokes to earn LeCarre a rematch on his own favourite surface, grass, i.e.

a courtroom. Actually 'court' works really well with the tennis analogy – grass court. Do you see what I'm saying? The word 'court' can be used when talking about tennis but also when talking about the law so it's a fantastic way of taking us from the tennis analogy and back into the world of criminal justice. This really is a very clever paragraph.

LeCarre banged his fist against Malone's door, loud enough so that it could be heard over Cardi B's latest supposed hit record. A woman who looked like she was probably called Tina – giant gold hooped earrings, a tube top, a bubble-gum bubble expanding out of her neon-red lipsticked mouth – opened Donkey's portal.

'You got a warrant?' Probable Tina was experienced enough to know LeCarre's face and savvy enough to know her rights.

'I just want to talk to Donkey,' said LeCarre.

'He's not here.'

'DONKEY! IT'S ROGER!' LeCarre shouted up the stairs of the two-bedroomed maisonette.

'LECARRE! Let him in, Tina.'

Donkey knew that there was no point turning away LeCarre, who could always find a warrant if he needed to. Besides, talking to the enemy was a good way of assessing what their priorities were, what was going on on their side of the criminal divide. These meetings served a purpose for both parties. LeCarre in the Benson Building was like Nixon in China, although the tennis analogy is probably a little stronger.

LeCarre crossed the threshold and into Donkey's avaricious abode.

'Shoes off, please,' said the young lady whose name was now confirmed as Tina.

LeCarre dutifully slipped off his Italian brogues. It may not have been to LeCarre's exquisite taste but it wasn't some rancid hovel. It was a nice place – couches of the finest white leather, marble counter tops, an original Van Gogh on the wall, or possibly a poster, he wasn't sure. What was clear was that crime paid.

Tina took LeCarre to Malone who was sat proudly on his replica throne puffing on a medium-sized cigar.

'Detective LeCarre! Take a seat, *mon ami*,' he said, open armed.

*Mon ami*? Did Malone speak French? It was this searing intelligence which had allowed him to rule the Exeter ghetto. Not that he was LeCarre's '*ami*'; he was his whatever the French is for foe.

'I see you've got some new furniture, Malone. Business good?' said LeCarre.

'Business is very good, Detective, thank you for asking,' said Malone.

'And remind me, Donkey, what *is* your business?' said LeCarre, fixing Malone with an interrogative stare.

'Don't tell me you've forgotten, Detective. I'm a window cleaner.' Malone deadpan smiled.

'I didn't know it paid so well,' said LeCarre, picking up a small solid gold statue of a lion.

'What can I say? I'm very good at what I do. I get those windows sparkling.'

'Charlie Fade? He clean any windows for you, Donkey?'

Donkey sat back, and took another puff of his American-made cigar. 'A few,' he answered, interested.

'Good worker was he, Donkey? This Fade. Good *window cleaner*?'

Just for the avoidance of doubt, they're not actually talking about window cleaning here – they're talking about crime.

'He was all right. Good kid. Maybe a little too good. Liked to talk,' said Malone.

'Liked to talk, huh? Is that why you killed him, Donkey? Didn't want him calling up Kelly and Baz on the Radio Exe breakfast show *Up With Kelly and Baz* and telling them all about your ... *window-cleaning business.*'

'Tell you the truth, LeCarre, I was a little more worried

91

about him talking to you,' said Malone. Why was he telling LeCarre about what could well be a motive for killing Charlie Fade? Could be a double bluff. Could very well be a triple. Donkey was a smart cookie – he was probably capable of anything up to an octuple bluff.

'So you killed him. Did it in the centre of Exeter on a Saturday night to send a message,' said LeCarre.

Donkey didn't blink. 'I didn't kill Charlie Fade, LeCarre.'

'No. But one of your minions did.'

Silence. Malone had clearly decided he'd said enough for the day. Maybe he had something to hide, maybe it was in his best interest to send LeCarre on a wild-goose chase. Thing was, Roger wasn't interested in catching a goose – he was interested in catching a murderer. LeCarre had one more question.

'Charlie Fade died on Saturday night, I'm sure you knew that.'

Donkey nodded.

'You got an alibi for Saturday night, Donkey?'

Donkey ran a hand over his clean-shaven head, cockily.

'I was washing my hair.'

LeCarre headed for the door.

'Oh, LeCarre, I forgot to say – congratulations on the award. Keeping us all safe you are, we really do appreciate it. Putting all those nasty criminals away.' Donkey was being sarcastic, like a guest on a Radio 4 satirical panel show. 'Of course, there is one villain you don't seem to be able to catch. Me.'

'Biding my time, Donkey. You'll get your turn.'

'How's the family?' said Donkey, mischievously.

'You keep the word "family" out of your mouth, renegade.'

'Only, I hear they've been going places they shouldn't really be going. Seeing people they shouldn't really be seeing. That Gasmask. It's got a lot of people going wild.'

LeCarre picked up the gold lion statue and threw it into Donkey's home bar, breaking several bottles. Tia Maria and Chambord raspberry liquor trickled down on to Donkey's engineered wood floor creating a sweet cocktail, but the atmosphere was anything but sweet.

'You don't know what the crap you're talking about. This is *my* city, Donkey,' said LeCarre. 'I can't *wait* until they build that Ferris wheel. One day I'm going to take a ride on that Ferris wheel, Donkey, and when I get to the top I'm going to look all around. I'm going to look up the M5 and see Taunton. I'm going to look east to Bridport, south to Torquay. I'm going to look over Dartmoor. They say it'll be so high that on a clear day you'll be able to see as far as

Liskeard. When that beautiful sunny day comes I'll survey Devon and Cornwall, my two counties, my patch, but you know what'll give me that nice warm feeling in my belly? It'll be what I can't see – Donkey Malone. Because Donkey Malone will be in his cell, *in prison*.'

# ELEVEN

Detective Roger LeCarre would soon be heading back into central Exeter, back into the metropolis, away from the dark and into the light, into a place with a future, but first he had someone to see in the squalor of the ghetto: Junior, son of his old dead partner Mick Lamb. LeCarre knew the maze of the Skibblemead Estate like the back of his hand and, thanks to the fact that he often wrote to-do lists and stuff on it, he knew the back of his hand very well indeed. Left, right, left, sharp right, under the bridge, through the passageway. Everywhere he looked were signs of decay – graffiti, crisp packets blowing across the path like salted tumbleweed, discarded shopping trolleys ... so many discarded shopping trolleys. You'd have thought the people here, living on low incomes as they did, would be keen to return their trolleys to retrieve the £1 deposit, but these people didn't care any more, they'd lost all hope. That's what happened when you got stuck in the 258th most dangerous council estate in Britain.

There it was, across a car park, through a sea of discarded shopping trolleys – the Rainbow Snooker Club. He knew Junior would be in there, looking for his pot of gold.

At 12.30 p.m. on a Monday afternoon, the Rainbow Snooker Club was pretty empty. Lights shone down on a couple of tables but other than that it was dark, mirroring the souls of its regulars. LeCarre stepped up to the counter, which was manned, as always, by Mickey Fix, a tobacco-stained fifty-year-old covered in tattoos. Mickey hadn't been seen outdoors since the 1980s. Legend had it he slept on table four.

'Morning, Detective.'

'Afternoon, Mickey.'

'Optics or fridge?' asked Fix, who knew his clientele well.

'It's a Monday lunchtime. Let's go fridge,' said LeCarre. 'Get me a Coors Light.'

The economics of the Rainbow Snooker Club were hard to compute. Tables were £5 an hour, a bottle of beer was £2.50. For most of the week, the number of patrons was in single figures. A place with that kind square footage should be bringing in a lot more cash. It was hard to see how

Mickey made it work. The Rainbow Snooker Club had to be a front for something. Perhaps this was where Donkey Malone was laundering his ill-gotten gains.

Save for the gentle soundtrack of balls hitting pockets, the joint was quiet.

'Junior here?' asked LeCarre, savouring his first unit of alcohol of the week.

'Always. Table fifteen.'

'Thanks, Mickey.'

LeCarre strolled over to Junior's table, the soles of his brogues struggling across the sticky carpet.

'Shouldn't you be at school?' said LeCarre.

Junior didn't look up. He was doing what he always did, potting balls.

'Teacher training day,' said Junior, quick as a flash. Junior was fourteen but looked twelve. Skinny, greasy, an awkward adolescent gait, he could be in a boyband if the boyband was manufactured with the sole intention of gaining sympathy for being ugly.

'Don't lie to me, Junior,' said LeCarre, picking a cue from the rack and expertly chalking it. 'I just passed your school. It's open.'

Everyone knew this was where Junior Lamb spent his days and truth be told it made sense. His school was so bad, learning the snooker trade gave him far better prospects. Few ever got out of Skibblemead but if they did, it was usually thanks to snooker. The Devon and Cornwall police force were supposed to be taking care of him and his mother, but you can't help a family that doesn't want to be helped. Anyone who's seen *Ramsay's Kitchen Nightmares* knows that. Since the death of Mick, Anne Lamb had fallen into a pit of daytime TV and Pernod. Unable to keep up with the mortgage repayments, they'd ended up on Skibblemead. LeCarre tried to take a positive interest in Junior. He could also be a good informer.

They were far enough away from the only other patrons for LeCarre not to be concerned about being heard.

'You know a kid called Charlie Fade? Bit older than you. He ever come in here?' asked LeCarre, while playing a smart safety shot that put Junior on the baulk cushion.

'Sometimes. Didn't play, though. Just came in some nights selling,' said Junior, attempting to return the cue ball to baulk but hitting the blue on the way back down and leaving LeCarre with a shot at a mid-range red.

'Selling what?' asked LeCarre, potting the red with a stun shot which held nicely for the pink into the opposite corner.

'You *know* what, Roger ... drugs,' said Junior, re-spotting the pink.

'What drugs?' said LeCarre, potting a red, screwing back off the side cushion with a touch of left-hand side and landing with a choice of three reds.

'You know, the usual.'

'What's the usual, Junior? Enlighten me,' said LeCarre, potting a red and leaving himself an angle on the black.

'Weed, pills, Gasmask.'

'Tell me you don't touch that stuff, Junior,' said LeCarre, powering the black into the corner pocket and using his phenomenal cue power to open up the pack of reds.

'I don't touch it,' said Junior, re-spotting the black. 'Except for maybe a little bit of weed from time to time.'

LeCarre miscued, missing his shot and standing up to look Junior in both of his eyes.

'What the crap did you just say?'

'Nothing,' said Junior, who already knew he'd revealed too much.

Junior reminded LeCarre of himself, except that LeCarre had been a lot better-looking as a teenager and had always had a stronger safety game. If Roger hadn't discovered his ability to solve crime, maybe he could have taken the wrong path. Growing up in Totnes with a mildly successful dentist father and a part-time ceramic artist mother, life wasn't easy for the young Roger LeCarre. Many times he'd looked at the River Dart and wished it could carry him away to a better place like Dartington or Buckfastleigh. He could still remember clearly the moment everything had changed for him. When the English teacher Mrs Batty had left the room for a moment, another child wrote Mrs Twatty on the blackboard. Mrs Batty returned and asked who'd done it. Having seen the crime take place, LeCarre put his hand up and said, 'Peter Atherton, miss!' Peter Atherton was rightly suspended and from that moment on Roger LeCarre was addicted to catching criminals. At break time he'd patrol the playground, looking for any minor infringement from a fellow pupil so he could tell the teachers. If another child ate a sweet in class, LeCarre would yell, 'Sweet! Illegal sweet!' The young Roger LeCarre trained himself to detect the rustle of a wrapper so quickly that the culprit could be caught before the sweet entered their mouth, thus denying them the pleasure of their crime.

For some reason Roger never made any friends at school. He always told himself that they were jealous of his crime-fighting skills but the truth may have been that it was LeCarre who put up the barrier – having friends complicated things when you had to hand them in to the authorities.

Like the remaining balls on the table, his head was all over the place. What did Donkey mean about his family? Was he just stirring the pot? Roger felt like he didn't know Carrie any more. Anything was possible. Was she on Gasmask? It could explain why she'd been acting so strangely, why she'd been pounding her way through the yogurts in the fridge at the alarming rate of more than one a day, why she'd stopped paying any attention to their favourite programme *Grand Designs*, why she'd spat on their marriage and had an affair with LeBron.

LeCarre didn't know. Domestic life was not his strength. Crime fighting was – it always had been, ever since he'd snitched on Peter Atherton. He needed to focus on what he did best. The domestic stuff would sort itself out, probably.

'You stay away from drugs, Junior,' said LeCarre, re-racking the table for another frame of the colourful game. 'I wanna turn on Eurosport 2 one day and see you competing in the Welsh Open, not go to work one day and find your outline in chalk.'

'Yes, Uncle LeCarre,' said Junior Lamb, who'd been in the ghetto long enough to pick up the working-class habit of calling people who aren't actually your uncle 'uncle'.

'So Charlie was dealing for Donkey, right?'

'S'pose so.' Junior shrugged and played a poor safety shot which left LeCarre with an opening for a tricky long red.

'Charlie have any enemies?' asked LeCarre, firing down the red from distance and leaving himself on the black.

'Don't think so; everybody liked him. Used to talk to everyone.'

'Who?'

'Me.'

'Who else?'

'Everyone. One night he'd be in here having a drink with Donkey's gang – Fizz, Beefy, Tonto, Graham – that lot. One night he was in the corner having a quiet one with a bloke in a suit.'

'What bloke in a suit?'

'Dunno. You gonna take your shot or what?'

LeCarre had still only potted the one red. Fourteen reds and the six colours remained. He had to get going, find Rhodes, see if the CCTV had come up with any leads. Heck, maybe the whole murder was on tape and they could chalk this case up as solved and go on a richly deserved holiday. LeCarre had always meant to walk the Cornish Coastal Path – perhaps now was the time. Of course, it wouldn't be that easy. It never was. LeCarre scored a quick 147, handed Junior a fiver and left.

# TWELVE

Rhodes had suggested they meet in some fancy coffee place called 'Costa' in the centre of town. Why couldn't they just meet in a pub like real men? Two p.m. and LeCarre had only had one beer. For the best, probably. Lately, he'd been finding it harder and harder to spit out mouthwash. He had to slow down.

LeCarre stood looking at the absurdly long menu.

'What do you want?' asked Rhodes.

Americano, Latte, Mochaccino. What did these words mean? It made about as much sense as this goddamn case.

'COFFEE! I thought this was a coffee place? Where's the coffee?'

'It's all coffee,' said Rhodes.

'Just . . . just get me a cup of chino,' said LeCarre, frustrated at how complicated the world had got. Back in the old days, everyone had a full English with a cup of tea for breakfast, a cheese and pickle sandwich with a Coke for lunch and a pork chop with mash and peas and two bottles of mild for dinner. Literally the whole country, every day. Simpler times. Now it was all about choice. Well, I choose to go back to the good old days, thought LeCarre, but that option doesn't seem to be on the menu.

They sat down. LeCarre took a sip of his cappuccino while Rhodes took out his 15-inch Dell laptop computer with Intel Celeron processor.

'Any luck in the ghetto?' asked Rhodes.

'There is no luck in the ghetto.'

'I've downloaded the CCTV footage, or what there is of it.'

'What there is of it?' asked LeCarre, taking another sip from his stupidly tiny cup of coffee. Seriously, he'd had two sips and it was half gone. Probably cost about £50 as well.

'There are two CCTV cameras pointed directly at where the murder took place, or at least where the body was found,' said Rhodes.

'Don't tell me. They weren't working,' LeCarre gruffed.

'They were working, both of them.'

'Then what's the problem?' asked LeCarre, leaning over and taking a weird-looking biscuit from Rhodes's saucer – he'd forgotten to eat.

'They both just happened to turn away from the scene of the crime at ten twenty-eight p.m.'

'Two minutes before the ten thirty p.m. to ten thirty-five p.m. timeframe given to us by Gita Patel,' said LeCarre, chewing and then spitting out the weird biscuit. 'How convenient.'

'That's right,' said Rhodes.

'So whoever did this had access to the CCTV operating system,' said LeCarre. 'Or at least they knew someone who did.'

'That's what I was thinking,' said Rhodes.

The two men looked at each other, a brief flicker of mutual respect. They may have taken different paths to reach the Devon and Cornwall police force, but they were both astonishingly smart.

LeCarre looked down at his Fitbit. His pulse was quickening; the caffeine had hit his bloodstream. Good. He needed to stay sharp.

'You said you had some footage. We're not going to watch a movie of a brick wall now are we, Rhodes? I suppose that's what you and your cap-and-gown boffins call an art film, is it?' LeCarre's interactions with Rhodes were gradually moving from outright bullying to something in the region of acceptable workplace teasing.

'No. I do have some footage of the fifteen or so minutes up to ten twenty-eight p.m. This at least gives us an indication of people who were in the area. People we might like to talk to,' said Rhodes.

'Our suspects,' said LeCarre.

'Sure, persons of interest. We can't be sure that the murderer passed through the square during that time. He may have only arrived when the murder took place,' said Rhodes, touching his glasses, like a nerd.

'The people who walked through the square are our suspects,' said LeCarre, emphatically.

'But, Detective . . .'

'Trust me. From now on, whenever we talk about this case, the people you're about to mention are our list of suspects.'

'Are you sure?'

'Yes. I have a hunch. My hunches are never wrong. I cannot emphasise this enough. *The list of people you are about to mention is our list of suspects for the murder of Charlie Fade.*'

'OK, shall I just list them all now? All the people who walked through the square where the murder took place in the preceding fifteen minutes?' asked Rhodes.

'Yes,' said LeCarre.

'OK. Right – Donkey Malone, Melanie Fade, Junior

Lamb, Rufus Scallion, Beverley Chang, LeBron Jax and Carrie LeCarre. Oh, and the comedian Josh Widdicombe.'

LeCarre downed his coffee. In the last twenty-four hours his wife had cheated on him, been revealed to be a possible drug fiend and become a suspect in the murder he was investigating. Next time he saw her they'd be having some serious words. He needed to talk to her anyway to see if she'd done anything about changing energy provider.

Roger and Rhodes ran through the eight suspects.

Donkey Malone: the most likely candidate. Criminal to his core. Although he'd never been convicted, the suspicion amongst the force was that he was no stranger to murder. Donkey had the means and, potentially, the motive. Fade sold drugs for him. Drug dealer was the most dangerous job on earth except for perhaps Alaskan sea fisherman, which LeCarre remembered seeing on a Discovery Channel documentary once. It could be as simple as Charlie messing up a stash and Donkey delivering the punishment like some kind of sickening postman. Had his fingers in every rotten pot in the city – could have easily crimed his way into gaining access to the CCTV.

Melanie Fade: Charlie's mother. What mother would kill her son? One who was caught up in Gasmask herself? Roger thought back to their afternoon of sensual delight, the way she'd swirled her head around like some kind of mad womanly propellor. Was she entirely stable?

Junior Lamb: the snooker-obsessed son of LeCarre's old partner. He knew Charlie, he'd admitted to that. Was he telling the full truth? Had they played a couple of frames one night, Charlie had won and suffered the consequences? Junior was known to be a bad loser from time to time. Sure, he was only fourteen but this generation was different. These days it was very rare for someone to get as far as sixteen in Exeter and *not* murder someone. LeCarre wasn't entirely sure on that statistic but it sounded right. The murder weapon was unusual, Gita had said. Could it be an extended spider, the kind used in snooker? Or maybe one of those weird ones that sort of extends over the top of the balls – a swan? Could he have used computer-hacking skills to turn the CCTV cameras away? All fourteen-year-olds are good at computer hacking.

Rufus Scallion: Exeter's inspirational new mayor. A member of the elite, what business would he have with a lowlife like Fade? Easy to see how the mayor would have access to the CCTV, though. He wanted to clean up the city, improve its reputation. Perhaps he had a plan to take out the criminals one by one. If that was the case then LeCarre admired his goals but not his methods. Criminals needed to meet justice the right way, not at the hands of some vigilante mayor. The movie *RoboCop* teaches us that however noble the beginnings, these things never end well. Besides, why just a little foot soldier like Fade? If cleaning up the city was Scallion's intention, then why not go straight for the head – Donkey Malone? As the CCTV showed, Donkey was in the area.

Beverley Chang: she wouldn't be the first criminal copper. Access to the CCTV wouldn't be a problem. Although she could be tough, Chang struck LeCarre as a mere ball breaker, not a life taker. The last time they'd met LeCarre remembered she'd been wearing a high-class fragrance – Yves Saint Laurent Opium, which every good cop knew cost £99 for 125 ml. Chief superintendents' salaries were good but were they *that* good? Did Chang have something going on on the side, something that went wrong perhaps? Something that led to the death of Charlie Fade?

LeBron Jax: if you can sleep with your best friend's wife then you can murder a nineteen-year-old in Exeter city centre. Even Hitler never slept with his best friend's wife. LeCarre had read a *lot* of Hitler biographies so he could be sure of that. The logical conclusion was that Jax was worse than Hitler and therefore capable of anything. But why would he have done it? The Chang corrupt copper theory could explain it, but could Jax really have been engaged in a criminal enterprise right under LeCarre's nose? LeCarre and Jax had spent the last couple of years in each other's pockets and it would seem that Jax had spent much of his little downtime screwing Carrie. LeCarre had already failed to detect the affair; if he had failed to detect Jax's taste for crime as well then maybe he wasn't the detective he thought he was. Perhaps LeCarre should pack it all in and become a wanderer, riding freight trains through the night, guitar on his back, a different lover in every town. He'd have to find some kind of sustainable revenue stream. He'd been meaning to find out what Bitcoin was for months.

Carrie LeCarre: if Carrie and LeBron were partners in the crime of extra-marital sex could they be partners in the crime of crime? Donkey had said something about his family 'going places they shouldn't really be going. Seeing people they shouldn't really be seeing'. He'd also implied she could be using Gasmask. When Roger had lifted the veil in St Stephen's church all those years ago, had he lifted the veil of a future murderer? It just seemed so far from the Carrie he knew. All those episodes of *Inspector Morse* they'd watched together, she'd never shown any indication of being on the side of the murderers. Carrie had always been behind Morse, 100 per cent. Or was that just a lie?

Like their whole marriage had been. Yes, over the course of their marriage Roger had slept with somewhere in the region of eighty to 120 women, but that was because he was in a highly stressed job. She, as far as he was aware, wasn't. The sickening CCTV footage showed Carrie and LeBron walking through the square holding hands. While Roger was getting drunk and eating KitKat Chunkies in a Premier Inn in preparation for visiting Mick Lamb's grave, they'd taken the opportunity for a date. *Just* a date? Zizzi's for dinner, murder for dessert? The simple fact was, along with Scallion and Chang, LeCarre had no evidence of any connection between Carrie and LeBron and Charlie Fade. That didn't mean there wasn't one.

Josh Widdicombe: Rhodes explained that Widdicombe was a so-called 'comedian' in Exeter for a tour show of his so-called 'comedy act'. LeCarre wasn't a fan of any of the new so-called 'comedians' and their so-called 'comedy'. What was wrong with proper jokes? Like the ones local racist comedian Cosmo told. Yes, they were racist but they were just jokes and he had a go at everyone, so what was the problem? All these new so-called 'comedians' were only interested in showing how 'clever' and 'alternative' they were. Maybe Josh Widdicombe had murdered Charlie Fade as some kind of 'alternative comedy joke'. Nothing would surprise Detective Roger LeCarre. Have you seen *Fleabag*? It's just filthy nonsense – not a joke in sight.

So those were their suspects, their pantheon of perpetrators, their slew of slayers, their extrapolation of executioners, their roster of rogues. LeCarre tried to see if he could think of one more – a schedule of scoundrels?

They seemed to be long on suspects but short on clues. Rhodes started to key his computer.

'What are you doing?' said LeCarre. 'We don't have time for Space Invaders. We've got a murderer to catch. The only space I want to be invading is theirs.'

'I'm finding out what *semper fidelis* means.'

*Semper fidelis*. The Latin phrase that was carved into Fade's body.

'That'll take hours to find out,' said LeCarre. 'We don't have time to take a Latin lesson.'

'*Always faithful*,' said Rhodes.

'What?'

'Always faithful. That's what *semper fidelis* means.'

Rhodes turned his laptop to LeCarre and showed him how to use Google. LeCarre couldn't believe it. The pen pushers from above were always trying to get them to use computers, which was ironic considering how much they loved pens, but LeCarre had always been resistant. 'You don't catch criminals on a computer,' he'd often say, to no one in particular. This Google, though – that was pretty impressive. It's not gonna be long before everyone's using this thing, thought LeCarre.

'Always faithful.' LeCarre let the words stew in his mind like a chicken casserole in his slow cooker. 'Faithful to what? *Faithful to what?*'

# THIRTEEN

'In my office, LeCarre, *now*!' said Chief Superintendent Beverley Chang for the second time that day. It was becoming a catchphrase. LeCarre had only gone back to the station to excrete his powerful afternoon coffee. From the look on Chang's face, his excretion was about to hit the proverbial fan.

'I've had a call from Donkey Malone,' said Chang.

'Lucky you,' snorted LeCarre.

'Less of the light-hearted banter, Detective,' said Chang. 'You're not Alexander Armstrong, I'm not Richard Osman and this sure as shit isn't the bit at the beginning of *Pointless* where they have a little chat with the contestants. Donkey says he had a visit from you today. Is that true?'

'Yes. Fade was working for Malone. I thought I'd give Malone a daytime quiz of my own.'

'Donkey says you smashed up his apartment. Did you?' said Chang. She was doing the quizzing now, like Bradley Walsh on *The Chase* or John Humphrys on *Mastermind* or Ben Shephard on *Tipping Point*.

'Smashed it up? That's an overstatement. I may have thrown something; it may have caused some damage. Don't blame the laws of force and motion on me. Blame Isaac Newton,' said LeCarre, intelligently.

'Dammit, LeCarre! You know damn well that's against the damn rules, dammit!'

Detective Roger LeCarre was the kind of copper who didn't play by the rules, except for the law of the land, which it was literally his job to uphold, and also the rules of sports and board games and stuff because as he often said to people, if you don't stick to the rules then there really isn't any point in playing. But other than that, LeCarre didn't play by the rules.

'This can't keep happening, LeCarre,' said Chang with her attractive mouth. 'Perhaps you need to go on a course.'

Another bloody course. You can't teach someone to be a copper – you're either born one or you're not. Everyone on the maternity ward can see the baby's a copper. What's the point of sending them to school or whatever it is babies do? If LeCarre had his way they'd hand the baby coppers a badge and a truncheon there and then and send them out on the streets to solve crime.

Chang walked out from behind her desk and made her way to the glass office wall that separated them from the station's open-plan office. LeCarre took in her expensive scent and her incredible figure. It was hard to decide whether he preferred her left leg or her right leg – both were stunning, housed as they were within long black stockings and stretching all the way down to her feet. LeCarre admired her from behind, but not in a creepy way, as she looked out over the assorted coppers sat at their desks.

'You're not like other police officers, are you, LeCarre?' said Chang from her unseen face.

'Aren't I?'

'I think you know you're not. If this is my zoo, out there I have my elephants, my monkeys, my zebras. But you, you're something different, Roger LeCarre.'

Chang slowly, sexily, turned the blind twisty thing that closes blinds – the wand? They were alone now. She rotated 180 degrees and faced LeCarre. As is often the case with women, she wasn't done talking.

'You have the intelligence of a dolphin, the killer instinct of a lion, the power of a rhino and yet somehow – you're all man.'

Was this a come on? Such was his libido, LeCarre tended to wear a condom at all times for moments such as these. With the recent ruptures in his marriage and the Fade case playing havoc with his usually highly functioning mind, Roger had forgotten to sheath today.

'Can I just ask a quick question?' said LeCarre. 'Are you pre- or post-menopause?'

'Post,' husked Chang, unbuttoning her blouse.

'Fantastic.'

LeCarre found the rapid switch from dressing down to undressing down arousing and became, like the largest Ferris wheel in Europe soon would be, fully erect. Within seconds Roger had added desk to the list of items of furniture he'd had penetrative sex on.

'Yes! Yes!' screamed Chang like a woman answering questions exclusively in the affirmative.

LeCarre watched a stapler gradually make its way closer to the edge of the desk with each thrust until it eventually tumbled recklessly to the ground. So spontaneous was the moment, so wild the energy in the room, that he didn't even break to pick the stapler up and put it back on the desk. Instead, Roger placed his hand on Chang's left breast, which was actually from his point of view her right breast, and slowly moved it around in a clockwise direction.

'Yes! Yes!' she screamed. Such was the power of LeCarre's sex, he'd reduced a woman with an IQ in the high 120s to a vocabulary consisting of one word. Being as they were, two employees of the state in a government-funded building during working hours, this was technically tax-payer-funded sex. If the tax payer knew the quality of the sex they were paying for they'd have no complaints, thought LeCarre.

He kissed her softly on the lips, then a little bit harder, then softly again. Chang wheezed with pleasure like an asthmatic masochist. LeCarre stepped up his piston-like thrusting to a steady rate of roughly 140 beats per minute and tried to think of something else to delay his lascivious emission. Perhaps now would be a good time to think about energy tariffs. For the past year he'd been on a dual fuel deal with E.ON and although the customer service left something to be desired, he'd been relatively happy with the monthly bills which he'd arranged to be paid by direct debit, smartly taking advantage of the discounted rate. Now his twenty-four-month tariff was coming to an end, it was sensible to shop around. With the possibility of a perma-nent split with Carrie, it was worth thinking about how the house could be empty more often – such a scenario might suggest looking for a deal with low-standing charges, rather than low per-kilowatt rates, although of course having both would be preferable.

Chang moaned with pleasure, exciting LeCarre who avoided climaxing by trying to see how many energy companies he could think of: E.ON, obviously, EDF, Scottish Power, British Gas, and wasn't there a renewable one called Octopus or something? If only LeCarre were an octopus now – that way he could caress every part of Beverley Chang's body at the same time. The thought aroused him. If they could plug their bodies into his house right there and then, they'd have been making enough dual fuel to power it for a year. He searched for another distraction.

Most of the papers on her desk were now on the ground – casualties of their lust – but some remained. With the frantic exercise in which he was engaged, it was difficult to focus. One sheet of paper caught his eye – a bank statement. Given it included some healthy deposits from the Devon and Cornwall police force, it would appear to be Chang's. LeCarre had never set his sights on reaching the force's top tier. He preferred to stay out on the streets, meeting crime where it was, rather than mixing with the elite. Chang's salary would be nice, though. Like a lot of red-blooded males, LeCarre liked to spend his summer holidays at the Elveden Forest Center Parcs near

Thetford in Suffolk. A detective's salary only stretched to a Woodland Lodge. From looking at Chang's balance, it would appear that on a chief superintendent's income he'd be able to afford a luxury treehouse complete with en suite bathrooms, hot tub and games room. But LeCarre was happy to stick with Woodland Lodges if it meant retaining his integrity and still having access to activities such as archery, kayaks and zip lining.

'Don't stop! Don't stop!' screamed Chang.

Something had grabbed LeCarre's attention, causing him to pause for a moment. He resumed thrusting while contemplating the new information. The Devon and Cornwall police force weren't the only organisation making deposits into Chang's account. There were two payments from something called DM Enterprises. DM. Donkey Malone? Was LeCarre currently copulating with the most sickening kind of person in the world – a dirty copper?

He looked into Chang's eyes. Were these the eyes of a traitor to the force? The only thing he could be sure of was that she was in sensual ecstasy. Was it deliberate? If she were playing for the other side, compromising the best cop on the force by loudly making love to him in the middle of the office at 4 p.m. on a Monday afternoon might be a smart move. Had Roger LeCarre just been played like something in a games room in a luxury treehouse lodge at Elveden Forest Center Parcs? His body was in rapture, but his mind was most certainly not.

They orgasmed in unison, LeCarre making a deposit of his own.


'I brought you in here to teach you a lesson,' said Chang, puffing on a post-coital vape minutes later. 'I didn't anticipate you teaching me one.'

'The pleasure was all mine,' suaved LeCarre.

'I think it's best we keep this between you and me, don't you think?' said Chang.

'I'm afraid that cat may have exited the proverbial bag ma'am,' said LeCarre. 'I think they probably heard us down in the Isles of Scilly, the archipelago just off the Cornish coast.'

Chang pointed to the walls. 'The office is fully sound-proofed, Detective.'

Interesting. Why were her walls soundproofed? Was that standard? Things were getting fishier than the Rick Stein programme LeCarre had on series record.

They were both fully clothed now. LeCarre headed for the door.

'Stay away from Malone, LeCarre,' said Chang.

'He's the biggest criminal on my patch. Staying away from him would be a dereliction of duty.'

'And allowing you to harass a citizen without evidence would be a dereliction of mine.'

'He was seen in the vicinity of the crime, just moments before it took place. I'd call that evidence,' said LeCarre.

'*Thin* evidence.'

Of course you would say that, thought LeCarre. *You're in the same goddamn boat.*

# FOURTEEN

Detective Roger LeCarre stood in his 40-square-metre penthouse apartment. Carrie hadn't called him and he sure as crap hadn't called her. He poured himself three fingers of maroon wine and sat on his stylish brown leather corner sofa. Quite the day. Chang's animal odour was still on him – the odour of a murderer?

At least he'd learned one thing that day – Google. What an incredible tool. If the criminals ever got hold of it, he'd be in trouble. He used it to quickly renew his TV licence, then legally turned on the television.

Five p.m. Time for *The Chase*. He'd watch *Pointless* later on iPlayer. As usual, LeCarre got every question right, yelling out the answer for no one in particular. But Bradley Walsh wasn't asking the questions that LeCarre really needed answers to.

Who'd tampered with the CCTV on Saturday night? Where was Donkey getting this new drug Gasmask from? Had Carrie really been hanging in the ghetto? Was Jax involved? Who were DM Enterprises? Was Chang on the take? Who killed Charlie Fade? Who killed Charlie Fade? *Who killed Charlie Fade?* The questions swirled around LeCarre's head like the clothes in his Zanussi A+++ rated washing machine.

Chang had told him to stay away from Malone. His wildcard mind told him that was exactly where he should go. Tomorrow, he'd sniff around the ghetto, see if Chang had her fingers in any rotten pies. If there was a connection between her and Malone then LeCarre had to be sure. Throwing around false accusations could spell the end of his distinguished career.

LeCarre's Huawei P30 Pro rang. Unknown number. Probably a cold call about PPI. LeCarre had successfully claimed his years ago. Wait ... the deadline for claiming PPI passed in August 2019. It must be something else. He answered.

'You're looking in the wrong places. You want to know who killed Charlie Fade but you're looking in the wrong places.'

The voice was low and robotic. Disguised.

LeCarre was as upright as the contestants on the now-muted *Chase*.

'Then where should I be looking?'

'Meet me at the top of the tallest building in Exeter in thirty minutes.'

LeCarre knew it well – the café at the top of John Lewis.

'How will I know who I'm looking for?' said LeCarre.

'I'll be wearing the county flower of Devon,' said the voice.

Of course, LeCarre knew the county flower of Devon. Every schoolboy within fifty miles knew the county flower of Devon.

'Primrose. I'll be there.'

Berlin, 1936. A young man by the name of Jesse Owens, through the simple act of running, proved Adolf Hitler and his theory of a master race wrong. Owens ran not just for gold, but for justice, too.

Nearly a century later, another man ran for justice. Justice for Charlie Fade. Detective Roger LeCarre running through the streets of central Exeter like a freight train through the Rocky Mountains, like a shark through the Caspian Sea, like a man on a mission. Leather jacket, brown brogues, moving at the speed of light – although technically a lot slower because that's physically impossible. Past Zara, past Clinton Cards, past Millets. It was like Roger LeCarre was a man made of metal and the world's largest magnet was pulling him in, dragging him to his destination, sucking him towards the truth, taking him to the café at the top of John Lewis.

He stood in front of the John Lewis facade and looked at his watch because he wanted to know the time. Fifteen minutes early. He probably could have just walked. Perhaps now would be a good time to pop in to Ryman's and stock up on stationery.

No.

Keep your head in the game, he told himself.

John Lewis sat at the top of the gentle hill that was Exeter High Street, a symbol of the city's status. The only John Lewis in the whole of Devon and Cornwall. At least Exeter had that. Looking down the High Street, LeCarre could see two branches of Waterstones. Two. On the same street. Sometimes LeCarre had to remind himself that although he spent his days and nights facing the city's darker side, Exeter still had a lot to be proud of.

Not every shop survived. Streamers, the famous party store, across the street from John Lewis, where every Exonian bought their balloons, had just been demolished. That spot had been chosen as the sight for the Great Rufus

Scallion Exeter Wheel. In terms of location it made sense. At the top of the city, it would be seen for miles around. It was sad to see the end of Streamers, though. The people of Exeter had something to celebrate but nowhere to buy party poppers. LeCarre shook his head at the irony and his thoughts returned to the matter at hand.

What if it was a trap? All he'd heard was a disguised voice. Why trust that voice? Any one of the shoppers walking in to John Lewis now could be an assassin. That elderly lady with a walking stick – could he be sure it was a walking stick and not an AR-15 encased in premium beechwood?

John Lewis would be closed soon. Was that part of the plan? Wait until everyone had left, shut the doors and take out Exeter's Person of the Year? Take out the one person most likely to catch you.

Suddenly LeCarre felt something he'd never felt before – vulnerable. Even just standing here outside John Lewis, amongst the thinning crowds. Perhaps they had him right where they wanted him. He scanned the roof of Next for snipers. He was a sitting duck. Wouldn't that be ironic? The man who chases murderers is himself murdered. Was that ironic? He was never 100 per cent sure on the definition.

You signed up for the police force, you signed up for risk. Heck, five of his partners had died – maybe it was his turn.

So be it. If he was walking to his death then at least he'd get to do so in one of the country's most iconic retail chains.

With any luck he'd be the first to arrive. That way he could assess the café for danger. He'd always felt that the John Lewis café made its tea far too hot. You had to wait twenty minutes before it was drinkable. Maybe now he could use that to his advantage – buy two teas and keep them as potential weapons should the need arise.

No point dwelling on the dangers any more. This could be it – his best chance to solve the case. Time to face the lift muzak.

LeCarre was about to turn and enter the revolving doors when something flashed before his eyes and landed on the Devon concrete with a thud. Screams came from passers-by. These were people on their way to M&S Food to take advantage of its stunning range of high-quality ready meals; now they were witnesses to a murder. Or was it just the aftermath of one? The body didn't move, the body didn't make a sound. Was it dead before it hit the ground?

'Stand back!' shouted LeCarre. 'Devon and Cornwall police force!'

He approached the cadaver – a young dead man in a suit staring skywards, towards his maker, and on his lapel . . . *a primrose.*

# FIFTEEN

'Long time no see,' Detective Roger LeCarre said to Laura Touch, humorously.

Just thirty-six hours earlier, they'd spoken at the crime scene of Charlie Fade. Now it was someone else's turn – Sebastian Twine, twenty-six, Capricorn.

'Another day, another body,' said Touch, like a tired sex worker.

'What have you got?' asked LeCarre.

'You were here first,' said Touch. 'You tell me.'

An almighty mess. That's what he had.

What looked like a solitary leaf blew along the high street until it got closer and LeCarre realised it wasn't a leaf at all but his new partner, Detective Tim Rhodes.

'You took your time, Rhodes,' said LeCarre.

'Sorry, Detective. My wife ... we were ... '

'Spit it out,' spat LeCarre.

'Antenatal classes. We're expecting a baby,' said Rhodes.

'Anti *what*? You're expecting a *what*?'

'Antenatal, sir. A baby, sir. We're expecting a baby. I'm her birthing partner,' said Rhodes, beaming with excitement.

'*Birthing partner?!* Are you listening to this, Touch?'

Touch rolled her lesbian eyes.

In LeCarre's world, births were nothing to do with the father. When Carrie had gone into labour with their daughter, LeCarre had sat in the Wonford Inn, the closest pub to the hospital. 'Text me when it gets here,' he'd said. Births were for doctors and midwives and mothers – they weren't for dads. Nine hours he'd waited. That day would always be remembered for two things – the arrival of his daughter and the most bags of pork scratchings he'd ever eaten in one sitting. When he eventually entered the hospital they'd had to give him hydration tablets because of all the salt in his system.

'What have we got?' asked Rhodes.

'Fell from the John Lewis café or, more likely, he was pushed,' said LeCarre.

'What makes you say that?' asked Rhodes.

'The giant stab wound might have something to do with it,' said LeCarre. 'Similar to Fade's. I received a call on my Huawei P30 Pro a couple of hours ago from someone claiming to have evidence on the murder of Charlie Fade. This is the man who I believe made the call.'

LeCarre went on to explain about the primrose, his plan of buying two hot cups of tea and his decision not to pop into Ryman's, which was closed now so he'd have to leave it for another day.

'Stab wound looks the same as Fade's, *semper fidelis* carved into his chest. It's the same killer. Come and take a look.'

LeCarre and Rhodes walked over to the body. Max Trescothick, the forensic, was outlining it in chalk. LeCarre hit him with some first-class police banter.

'You ever think of drawing something else, Trescothick?'

'Shouldn't you be *drawing* your pension, you old bugger?' Trescothick hit back, ruthlessly.

LeCarre searched for a retort. 'I think it'll be back to the *drawing* board if . . . '

The witty back-and-forth was interrupted by Rhodes vomiting on the corpse.

'Oh my God! That's Seb Twine!'

LeCarre looked to his pathetic puking partner.

'Sorry,' said Rhodes. 'It's just, I was wondering why he wasn't at the antenatal class tonight.'

'Oh dear. When was the baby due?' asked Trescothick, wiping Rhodes's vomit from the corpse.

'Just a couple of weeks, I think. He was so excited. Caroline . . . poor Caroline!'

Poor Caroline indeed. Sebastian Twine should have been putting together a flat-pack cot. Now someone would be putting together a flat-pack coffin. He should have been fitting a stair gate, not waiting at the pearly gates. New fathers should be losing sleep, not sleeping for eternity.

'Tell me about Twine, Rhodes. Was he mixed up in something he shouldn't have been mixed up in?' asked LeCarre.

'I don't think so. He just seemed liked a lovely guy. Loved his wife, loved his job.'

The whole thing was a tragedy. Like *Othello* by William Shakespeare, or *King Lear*, which is also by William Shakespeare.

'And what *was* his job, Rhodes? What did Sebastian Twine do?' asked LeCarre.

'He worked for Exeter City Council. He worked for Rufus Scallion.'

Nine a.m. The following day. Tuesday. Rufus Scallion was already in his council chambers, going over some briefing papers and eating from a large bowl of roasted chicken legs. He was, to the surprise of Detectives LeCarre and Rhodes, dressed in full ceremonial garb.

'Gentlemen. Please, take a seat. Chicken leg?'

LeCarre and Rhodes took Scallion up on the offer of a seat, but not poultry. For LeCarre, chicken was very much a post-midday meat. Come to think of it, for him, pork was probably the only 'round the clock' meat.

'You're probably wondering why I'm in the robes. Most people assume I wear a simple suit when not at official events,' said Scallion. 'The robes provide me with an important reminder of the responsibilities of my office. I'm not the first mayor of Exeter and I won't be the last. These robes, they've been worn by every mayor of Exeter for the last thousand years – they symbolise the proud history of the role and, by extension, this city.'

'I quite understand, Mayor Scallion,' said LeCarre. 'For similar reasons I always go to bed with a taser strapped to my leg. I've had a couple of accidents but it is, as you say, an important reminder.'

Scallion lifted one of his heavy velvet sleeves and wiped chicken grease from his moustache.

'I expect you're here about Sebastian. I was told the news last night. Such a tragedy.'

'Did you know Sebastian well, Mayor Scallion?' asked LeCarre.

'How well does any man know another?' asked Scallion. 'Aren't we all just dirty laundry, tumbling through life's spin cycle, hoping to come out clean?'

Rufus Scallion was Roger LeCarre's kind of man – capable of saying things which sounded incredibly profound even when, on deeper analysis, they didn't really make all that much sense.

'How long had he worked for you?' asked Rhodes.

'A couple of years. He was a very talented young man. You could name any property in Exeter and Sebastian would immediately tell you what council tax band it was in.'

LeCarre was impressed. It was a skill he'd been working on acquiring himself.

Scallion stood up and walked over to one of the room's large windows. The Exeter City Council offices were just across from the bus station and a few metres from where Streamers had sat only a week before. On becoming mayor the first thing Scallion had done was personally clean his new workplace's notoriously grubby brutalist facade. Doing it all by himself, it took him a month but it was his way of showing the city he meant business. Scallion looked down on the beginnings of the giant Ferris wheel which would soon bear his name.

'In many ways I blame myself for what became of Sebastian. I should have put a stop to it. This city – it has to stop eating its sons.'

'Put a stop to what?' asked LeCarre.

Scallion turned his head back to LeCarre at roughly 20 mph, which is quite a fast movement for a head.

'You didn't know?'

'Know what?'

'Sebastian was mixed up in the underworld. At least, that was my assumption. I couldn't prove it, I'm not a police officer, I'm not Detective Roger LeCarre, I'm not Exeter's Person of the Year.'

LeCarre bristled. Was Scallion suggesting there was something he should have worked out by now? Was he questioning his skills of detection? No one had done that since Carrie had complained when Roger couldn't locate the source of a smell in their family car. Maybe that incident was the first sign of trouble in their marriage. In the end they'd had to burn the car, only for LeCarre to remember he'd put some smoked mackerel in the glove box three months before.

'What makes you think Sebastian Twine was involved in the underworld, Mayor?' asked LeCarre.

'Sebastian was, as I say, very talented and until a few

months ago he was a good worker. He was very much involved in the planning for our stint as UK Capital of Culture. I'd told him to go out there and find up-and-coming musicians and the like – people who could bring something to the festivities. I think he may have taken on the role a little too enthusiastically, Detective. Every night he'd be off to an event – some indie band gig, some gallery opening, some poetry slam. Christ knows what his darling wife Caroline thought. He'd always been very punctual but he started coming in at ten minutes past, a quarter past nine. You can't have your staff coming in late; that's no way to run a council.'

'I can see why that could have affected his work. But the underworld?' said LeCarre. 'It just sounds like he was having a little too much of a good time.'

'Does the word *drugs* mean anything to you, Detective?'

LeCarre clenched his fist.

'I have reason to believe Sebastian was taking part in *drugs*. I found *this* on his desk one day.' Scallion was suddenly holding a two-foot-high bong.

'That's quite the piece of apparatus,' said LeCarre. 'If you don't mind, we'd like to take that as evidence. But, Mayor Scallion, Sebastian Twine wasn't killed by drugs. Sebastian Twine was murdered.'

'Detective, I, like you I'm sure, keep my ear to the ground. It is my understanding that Sebastian had become involved with Donkey Malone.'

Donkey Malone. Everything led to Donkey Malone, and yet Chang had told LeCarre to leave him alone. The story made sense – Charlie Fade had done something to upset Donkey. Upset a Donkey and you're liable to get hurt. Sebastian Twine had found himself part of that world, getting drugs from Donkey's gang, perhaps even dealing some on the side to pay for his antenatal classes. Twine knew what had become of Fade. The streets of Exeter lived by a code – no snitching – but Twine wasn't from the streets. He was from the cul-de-sacs. A middle-class kid with a steady job who'd been to one too many poetry slams and found himself on the wrong side of the tracks. Twine may have had drugs pumping through his veins but there was something else in his blood, too – a conscience. He'd called LeCarre to give him the vital piece of evidence that would send Donkey down but donkeys' ears are closer to the ground and Donkey had found out. Donkey killed Twine before Twine could tell LeCarre that Donkey had killed Fade.

*You're looking in the wrong places* – that was what Twine had said on the phone. But how did Twine know where

LeCarre was looking? LeCarre had been to see Donkey Malone. Surely he'd been looking in the *right* place? Perhaps Twine was warning LeCarre away from the rest of his suspects: Chang, Jax, Carrie, Melanie, Scallion and Josh Widdicombe. Telling him to go back to Malone – stay on track. It was like the smell in the car all over again. It was probably the case that tormented LeCarre the most. He'd spent days ripping out the upholstery, tearing apart the car, when the problem was in the most obvious place all along – the glove box. Donkey Malone was the glove box.

Not that LeCarre had a damn shred of evidence. This was all still just like climate change, thought Roger – a nice theory, but with absolutely no hard evidence to back it up.

LeCarre's thoughts were interrupted by the sound of construction. It was just twenty-four hours since work had begun and the Ferris wheel was already taking shape. Scallion turned back to look at it with pride.

'I hope you don't take this the wrong way, Detectives, but I plan to put you out of business,' said Scallion.

LeCarre raised one eyebrow. 'Is that so, Mayor Scallion?'

'To you my Ferris wheel may look like a giant circular lump of metal, a mere monument, a simple ride.'

'Is it something else, Mayor?' asked Rhodes, who both Scallion and LeCarre had forgotten was there.

'It's a space rocket, gentlemen.'

LeCarre's left eyebrow was no longer the only raised eyebrow in the room.

'Once the youth of Exeter step on to my Ferris wheel, once they get to the top and view the distant horizon, there'll be no ceiling to what they can achieve, no limit to how far they can go.'

Oh, I get it – it was a metaphor, thought LeCarre.

'When you can get as high as *that*, gentlemen,' said Scallion, 'you won't need to lower yourself to crime.'

LeCarre had spent his life trying to eradicate crime. Maybe the mayor had got there before him. Maybe this was the solution – a giant Ferris wheel that showed the citizens a better way. There was a big Ferris wheel in London, of course, the London Eye. Was there still crime in London? LeCarre made a mental note to find out on Rhodes's Google.

'I do hope I was able to be of some help,' said Scallion.

'You were, Mayor,' said LeCarre. 'A great deal, thank you.'

'Will I be seeing you at the Capital of Culture celebrations, Detective LeCarre? You're our Person of the Year. You simply have to be there.'

'I will if time allows, Mayor.'

'What could possibly get in the way of such a joyous evening, Detective?' said Scallion.

'*Crime.*'


LeCarre and Rhodes were walking back to Roger's Kia Ceed when he received a phone call from Gita Patel, the pathologist. She got straight to the point.

'We've found something on Sebastian Twine.'

'Same stab wound, *semper fidelis* carved into the chest, I know – same killer,' said LeCarre.

'No. We found something else, in his wallet: a receipt for the Edinburgh Woollen Mill from last week.'

'So he went to the Edinburgh Woollen Mill. I go there all the time. The guy obviously had good taste in scarves,' said LeCarre, impatiently. Women! They always wanted to talk about shopping.

'No, Detective LeCarre, you don't understand,' said Patel. 'The receipt wasn't from the Exeter branch of the Edinburgh Woollen Mill.'

'Then what branch was it, Patel?'

'New York.'

LeCarre hung up, frantically. 'Get in the car.'

'What is it?' said Rhodes.

'GET IN THE CAR!' LeCarre was already revving up the engine. Rhodes got in.

'You got your passport on you, Rhodes?'

'Yes. I always have my passport on me. It's the first thing we were taught at police training school.'

'Good,' said LeCarre.

'Why?'

'*We're going to New York.*'

# SIXTEEN

The Boeing 777 took its first flight in 1994. Tonight it would take its most important – Exeter Airport to JFK. Detective Roger LeCarre reclined his first-class seat and applied a warm towel to his face. He needed to be at his best. What was Sebastian Twine doing in New York? This receipt from the Times Square branch of the Edinburgh Woollen Mill – this could be the thing that blew the whole damn case open.

'And you're sure I'll get the money back on my next pay cheque?' Detective Rhodes was still going on about LeCarre making him put the flights on his credit card. 'It feels like we should have run this by Chang first.'

'Don't be such a wimp, Rhodes,' said LeCarre, looking through the film choices.

'I don't mean to be ... it's just with the baby and

everything, two first-class flights bought at the airport . . . it's about half a year's salary.'

'Trust me, it'll be fine. I need you to pay for the hotel when we get there too, by the way. Sorry, I would get it myself but I'm in the middle of changing energy tariff so I'm not 100 per cent sure where my finances stand,' said LeCarre, now flicking through the watches in the duty-free magazine.

'I think I might need to take out a loan,' whinged Rhodes.

'Don't worry. This trip is courtesy of the Devon and Cornwall police force. You can't put a price on solving crime.'

This wasn't the first time LeCarre had taken one of his investigations international. A couple of years back, a man suspected of fly-tipping had disappeared on a two-week holiday to the Seychelles. Desperate to close the case, LeCarre had followed the suspect out there and brought him back in handcuffs. Ultimately it proved to be a case of mistaken identity and the man was acquitted but LeCarre never regretted pursuing every lead in the battle against crime.

The ice in LeCarre's drink rattled as the aircraft accelerated down the runway. The ice wasn't the only thing that was rattled – Detective Tim Rhodes looked rattled, too. In

Rhodes's hand was not a drink or a magazine but a sick bag which was filling up quickly.

'We're not even in the air yet!' said LeCarre.

'Sorry, I'll be fine once we're through the clouds.'

This new partner was wetter than LeCarre's Southern Comfort and lemonade. LeCarre put on some headphones and looked for a movie starring Denzel Washington. If there was ever a film made of LeCarre's life, he had Washington in mind for the role. There were few actors who'd be able to capture his blend of masculinity, sensuality and trivia knowledge, but Washington seemed to fit the bill.

Rhodes now had an eye mask on and appeared to be asleep. Good, thought LeCarre. He might need the rest. New York was sometimes referred to as the 'city that never sleeps', which LeCarre had always found odd because obviously the people in the city *do* sleep. Was it simply a reference to some shops being open twenty-four hours? There was a twenty-four-hour Tesco in Exeter now so you could call Exeter the city that never sleeps too if you really wanted to.

Perhaps LeCarre should get some rest as well. The queue for the bathroom had subsided. He went to make a quick visit before closing his eyes across the North Atlantic Ocean.

As soon as he opened the folding toilet door he could smell that a crime had taken place. Tobacco. Someone had just smoked a cigarette and flushed it down the lavatory. As quick as the evidence must have disappeared through the powerful flushing system, LeCarre found himself in a rage. He stepped out into the cabin, grabbed the PA and made an announcement.

'This is Detective Roger LeCarre. I'm commandeering this flight to New York on behalf of the Devon and Cornwall police force.'

A flustered air stewardess approached.

'Can I help, sir?'

'Somebody broke the law. I need to find out who.' LeCarre spoke into the tannoy again. 'A passenger on this plane just smoked a cigarette in the toilet. According to the sign in there, that carries a fine of up to twenty-five thousand dollars. We can do this the easy way or the hard way – whoever did it can come up here and hand themselves in, or I can ask the captain to turn this hundred-and-fifty-ton chunk of metal around and take us back to Exeter. So what's it gonna be?'

'Sir, I really don't think you have the authority to do this.'

'We may be over international waters but the law is the law and crime is crime.'

No one was forthcoming. LeCarre was back on the tannoy.

'All right. Looks like I'm going to have to start searching bags. My apologies to the law-abiding passengers amongst us.'

LeCarre powered his way down the aisle, opening overhead baggage bins. Rhodes frantically grabbed hold of him.

'Roger, what are you doing?'

'Go back to sleep, Rhodes. I've got everything under control. Looks like we might be headed back to Devonshire.'

A more senior flight attendant approached LeCarre. 'Sir, I'm going to have to ask you to sit down.'

'And I'm going to have to ask you to tell the captain to turn around because this aircraft is currently transporting a criminal to the United States of America.'

Now the pilot was approaching. 'Sir, I need you to sit down.'

'Good evening, Captain. I don't tell you how to fly planes, do I? So don't tell me how to do my job.'

Roger LeCarre had dramatically changed the mood of nearly four hundred people in just three minutes.

'Roger.' Rhodes had fixed LeCarre with a glare. 'Roger, I need you to listen to me.'

'You've got twenty seconds, Rhodes. Twenty seconds before I get myself into the cockpit and work out how to fly this jumbo jet on my own.'

'A crime has taken place,' said Rhodes.

'You're damn right it has!' yelled LeCarre.

'But that's not the crime we're here to solve.' Rhodes was speaking with a calm confidence Roger hadn't seen before. 'Right now, we're here to get justice for Melanie Fade, for Caroline Twine. However evil the crime that occurred in that toilet was, turning this plane around will not help us to find out who killed Charlie Fade and Sebastian Twine. Do you see what I am saying, Detective LeCarre?'

'Yes. Yes, I suppose I do. In a way.'

LeCarre's Fitbit detected his heart rate dropping back to a normal level. Rhodes handed LeCarre an eye mask.

'Why don't you sit down and get some rest?'

'OK ... OK.'

# SEVENTEEN

New York City – twinned with Exeter, if not in actuality, then in spirit. Two throbbing metropolises, two monuments to the achievements of man, two hotbeds of crime.

This was Detective Roger LeCarre's first time in America. Before he'd even left the airport he knew he was in no ordinary country. Signs with slightly different spellings, not a single branch of WHSmith, toilet bowls where the water went nearly all the way up to the rim – it was like he'd stepped on to another planet. Two NYPD cops stood near the exit, guns in holsters, thumbs in belt loops. LeCarre gave them a nod and they each nodded back. The brotherhood of copdom transcended continents.

For a brief moment, LeCarre doubted himself. Now he was a big fish in a bigger pond, he had to be on the lookout for sharks. But then, as the saying goes, if you can make it in Exeter, you can make it anywhere.

LeCarre and Rhodes left JFK arrivals and hopped into a yellow taxi cab, not an item of luggage between them.

'Take us to the Edinburgh Woollen Mill, Times Square.'

'You got it, buddy,' said the taxi driver, in an unmistakable American accent. 'Edinburrow Woollen Mill, here we come.'

LeCarre tensed at the driver saying 'Edinburgh' in that stupid way that Americans do. It was strange to hear people talking in genuine bona fide American accents. Deep down, LeCarre had always assumed it was something they put on for movies. But no, they really did talk like that.

'I wonder if we'll see the Empire State Building,' said Rhodes, excitedly.

LeCarre narrowed his eyes to the size and shape of flattened raisins. 'We're not here to sightsee, Rhodes.'

'I know. It's just I've never been to New York before. Marisa Tomei is in a production of *Death of a Salesman* on Broadway. I hear her performance is spellbinding.'

'Rhodes. We're going straight to the Edinburgh Woollen Mill, we're asking some questions and then we're heading back home.'

'But you mentioned a hotel.'

'Well, we'll see. A case is like a train – you go where it takes you. I don't think it's gonna take us to *Death of a Salesman*, Rhodes, I'm sorry.'

LeCarre and Rhodes stepped out of their yellow travelling chamber and into the pulsating madness of downtown Manhattan. Was there anywhere on earth quite like Times Square, except for Piccadilly Circus and probably somewhere in Tokyo? The two men spun around, taking in the enormous billboards, all the crowds, until they became dizzy.

'Hot dogs! Get your steaming hot dogs here! Fresh from the fryer!' shouted a street vendor.

Everywhere you looked were breakdance crews, contorting their young bodies to the latest foul-mouthed jam. To their left Spike Lee was shooting a movie, to their right an incredibly overweight man was eating a bagel. The whole vista screamed 'New York!' They steadied themselves and entered the Edinburgh Woollen Mill.

In what was, on reflection, an unsurprising development, the staff had no memory of a young British man entering the store nearly two weeks ago.

Kaplinsky's Bar, at the corner of 8th and Fitz. Detective Roger LeCarre nursed a Jameson on the rocks, Rhodes a pineapple juice. With no flights back to Exeter until the following day, the two men had decided to take a bite out of the Big Apple – see if they couldn't find some info on their friend Sebastian Twine.

On the TV, the New York Knicks were playing the LA Dodgers – LeCarre never did understand the appeal of ice hockey – 'Quarter Backs' and 'touchdowns' – none of it made any sense.

The jukebox was playing 'Born in the USA'. Roger LeCarre was anything but, but he looked right at home. Jet-black hair, stubble – he could be a cop from the Bronx, unwinding after a tough day on the block.

'Can I get you two anything to eat?' asked the barman.

'Do you do a ploughman's?' asked LeCarre.

The barman shook his head.

'Then I think we'll leave it, thank you, mate.'

Kaplinsky's was your typical American cop bar. Have you seen *The Wire*? Picture one of the bars in that. Shamrocks, sports memorabilia, a weary bartender cleaning a glass.

'Come on!' yelled the burly moustachioed bald cop at the bar beside them. 'Get the goddamn puck into the end zone!'

'I think we're about ten minutes from the theatre,' said Rhodes. 'If we leave now we'll make curtain up.'

LeCarre ignored him. He admired Marisa Tomei as much

as anyone but they weren't there to take in a Tony-winning Arthur Miller reprisal, they were there to solve a crime. Roger leaned towards the bald cop.

'Say, can I buy a fellow boy in blue a drink?' said LeCarre, instantly worrying that the sentence sounded a little camp.

'Sure,' said the moustached cop. 'Detective Mac Mullally, NYPD.'

'Detective Roger LeCarre, Devon and Cornwall police force. This is Detective Tim Rhodes.'

The men shook hands. Men. Shaking hands. In a bar in New York. It didn't get much better than this.

'Barman! Three of your finest drinks, please,' said LeCarre.

'Devon and Cornwall, huh? I hear you guys got it pretty rough,' said Mullally.

He knew their patch. That felt good.

'You could say that,' said LeCarre. 'Crime is a gas. It seeps into every pore.'

'Ain't that the truth.' Mullally raised his glass and the men clinked.

Over the course of the next hour, a bridge was built across the Atlantic Ocean. It didn't matter where they came from – cops were cops. Mullally told the story of the first school shooting he was ever called to and LeCarre spoke

152

of the time he caught his able-bodied dentist parking in a disabled space at ASDA. Tragically, both incidents had ended in a fatality.

Taking a long shot, Rhodes asked if Mullally had come across a man by the name of Sebastian Twine in the last month. Negative. Maybe Twine's visit had been a simple vacation, a trip away before becoming a father, thought LeCarre. But Twine's reported descent into the Exeter underworld had to be connected to his death – it seemed unlikely that his trip to New York wasn't too. Could they be sure Twine even went to New York? Perhaps the killer had planted the Times Square Edinburgh Woollen Mill receipt to throw them off the scent. This case was as tangled as the pretzels the men were chewing on.

'So how's things in your parish right now?' asked Mullally. 'Busy?'

'You know how it goes,' said LeCarre. 'A new drug hits the streets and everyone starts scrambling for position – like linebackers in the ninth inning.'

'Ain't that the truth,' said Mullally for the second time in the conversation. 'Dalliance. That's what they're calling it, our new chemical nightmare. Been with us for a year now.'

The men compared notes.

'Gasmask for us,' said LeCarre. 'One hit and they say

you feel like a piece of paper folding into an origami swan. Sounds great until the wind picks up and you're blown away.'

'Say,' said Mullally. 'I don't know this Twine guy, but if his visit to New York was something to do with something shady then he probably went to Stallion.'

'Stallion?' said Rhodes.

'It's Manhattan's most popular nightclub and the epicentre of the New York mafia. All crime in this city flows through Stallion. I gotta start my shift soon but I can take you two cats there first if you like.'

'We like,' said Detective Roger LeCarre.

# EIGHTEEN

Five hundred bodies under five thousand beams of light reflecting off one disco ball moving to the modern American beat. Detective Roger LeCarre hadn't been to a nightclub since LeBron Jax's stag do ended at Majestics in Newquay. Stallion was a whole different ball game. Popular with surfers, the dance floor at Majestics, Newquay, had been full of wetsuits. At Stallion, it was all expensive American silk shirts and tight-fitting dresses.

The eyes of the Stallion clientele were the most striking thing. Their bodies were in Harlem but their visual organs were somewhere else entirely. Jacked up on Dalliance, that new narcotic Detective Mac Mullally mentioned towards to end of the last chapter.

It was tragic to see people waste their youths on drugs. Could LeCarre really judge? Much of his younger years had been dedicated to online Scrabble. His mid-twenties were a blur. Hour upon hour spent agonising over having a Q but not a U and underutilised triple-word squares. Had he been in any less of a haze than the drooping faces and frantic limbs he saw before him now?

He often wondered if his Scrabble days had affected his work. Sure, he'd got himself to the top fifty in the south-west of England, but could he have caught the Bideford Butcher, Devon's most notorious serial killer, if the butcher's brutal spree hadn't coincided with the height of LeCarre's Scrabble addiction? Maybe. No use dwelling on it now. The Butcher's victims, like LeCarre's online Scrabble reputation, were dead.

Mullally handed LeCarre and Rhodes two ice-cold bottles of the American beer 'Budweiser', fresh from the refrigerator. LeCarre took a sip.

'Not bad. You don't get *that* in Exeter.'

Maybe the trip had been worth it after all.

'So what's the game plan?' asked Rhodes, geekily placing his Budweiser down like some kind of nerd. 'We're here for information. Shall we just start asking around?'

LeCarre and Mullally let out a hearty shared laugh.

'Where did you get this kid?' asked Mullally.

'Leicester De Montfort University,' said LeCarre.

'Ain't that the truth,' said Mullally for literally the third time in about an hour.

'We need to blend in, Rhodes. We can't just start asking questions, we're not Rick Edwards on the BBC One quiz show *Impossible*,' said LeCarre. 'They'll know we're D and C Police straight away.'

The men formulated a backstory. It was decided that LeCarre and Rhodes were twins, up from Mississippi to blow off some steam before they married a pair of twin-sister tennis pros. Rhodes wondered whether they could pull it off.

'Wouldn't it be easier to just say we're friends from England? We don't look alike and I'm not confident I can do an American accent.'

'You better get confident quick,' said LeCarre. 'If you can't go undercover, you can't police.'

Undercover work was one of Detective Roger LeCarre's many specialities. In another life he probably could have been a VAT-registered actor. For six months he'd success-fully infiltrated a Jamaican Yardie gang by winning the trust of the leader and becoming his girlfriend. Luckily he'd managed get the information needed for a conviction before he was in too deep and feelings became involved.

'Listen, I know you limey cops do things differently but I

wouldn't feel comfortable letting you out into the field without a piece,' said Mullally, handing LeCarre and Rhodes a gleaming Glock 19 each because 'piece' means gun.

'Shouldn't we have some kind of training first?' asked Rhodes.

LeCarre looked down in embarrassment. His partner was a square.

'If a bad guy comes for you, you point your pistol at them and shoot. Congratulations. You just completed basic training. You passed with flying colors,' said Mullally, saying colours with the American spelling.

'No, but seriously,' said Rhodes, 'I've never even held a gun before. I literally don't know where the safety is.'

'Just stick it in your waistband and hit the dance floor,' said LeCarre. 'We've got work to do. Are you joining us, Mac?'

'I'm sorry, gentlemen. I was supposed to be at my precinct, which is American for police station, an hour ago.' Mullally looked each of the two Brits in the eye. 'LeCarre. Rhodes. You stay safe out here, all right?'

'Safe? I don't know the meaning of the word,' said LeCarre, even though he obviously did.

Detective Roger LeCarre moved his body in synch to the rhythm. Like a pregnant woman and her baby, he and the music were one – but who was gestating whom? At first, he'd simply imitated the movements of the other dancers, now he was just another one of them giving in to the visceral energy of Ed Sheeran's latest hypnotic creation. But LeCarre wasn't there to dance. He was in a Harlem nightclub for one very simple reason – to find out who pushed Sebastian Twine out of the window of the Exeter John Lewis café.

Beside him, a Latino woman in a leopard-print dress moved her hips from side to side, east to west. She looked like Jennifer Lopez but with bigger breasts and a slightly bigger nose.

'Baby, I like the way you move,' she whispered loudly to LeCarre.

'The feeling is mutual, ma'am,' said LeCarre in a perfect Mississippi drawl. 'This here be my twin brother, we up from Mississippi for a good time an' we sure is havin' it.'

'Country boys, huh? Welcome to New York. The city that never sleeps.'

'City that never sleeps. I like that,' said LeCarre. 'I heard the same said of a city in England called Exeter. They say they gotta Tesco that's open twenty-four hours a day. Hoooo-wee!'

'Exeter? Where did I hear of that place?' The 6 foot 6 woman searched her Latino mind. 'Oh yes, that's right. I met a guy from Exeter here last week. Nice guy. He told me that city is gonna build the biggest Ferris wheel in Europe.'

LeCarre and Rhodes looked at each other. The guy she spoke of could be Sebastian Twine.

'Oh yeah?' said LeCarre, wishing he hadn't chosen to do a Mississippi accent and wondering if there was a way he could just slowly transition back into his own voice. 'You met a guy from Exeter, huh? What was he doing here, just out of interest?'

'Sebastian?'

It was Sebastian.

'I'm not sure but he spent some time with Julius. I think he was here on business, if you know what I mean.'

'Julius? Who's Julius?' said Rhodes, completely forgetting to do the accent.

'Julius? You don't know Julius? He's the guy who runs this joint, runs half this city. My pimp and the inventor of Dalliance.'

Considering she was just a random woman on the dance floor and the first person they'd spoken to, the conversation had been remarkably productive.

'*I can introduce you to him if you like.*'

# NINETEEN

The back office, Stallion nightclub, Harlem, New York City, New York, USA, North America.

Two detectives from the Devon and Cornwall police force sat on a crocodile leather couch waiting to meet Julius Ramone, the most powerful gangster on the East Coast. Some might say that two armed British detectives managing to get alone in a room with such a man with almost zero effort isn't really believable but it did definitely actually happen.

Detective Roger LeCarre placed a Trebor Extra Strong mint on his tongue and let the intense flavour numb his senses. He looked up at the crystal chandelier hanging from the gold-plated ceiling. Crime paid, that was for sure. He steadied himself by going through the exercises his sensei had taught him. Breathe in, breathe out. This wasn't Julius's territory. It was Detective Roger LeCarre's.

'Follow my lead,' LeCarre growled at Rhodes.

First they saw the cowboy boots, then the python draped over a pair of shoulders, then the gold-toothed smile of Julius Ramone.

'Sorry, gentlemen. I wuz just gittin' ma dick sucked.'

Ramone's voice was as gravelly as LeCarre's driveway. This wasn't some cartoon racial stereotype from a poorly researched genre novel written in British suburbia – this was a real-life New York gangster in the flesh. LeCarre used his masculinity to find a common ground.

'From one red-blooded man to another, I have to say, I quite understand.'

LeCarre was now speaking in his native British accent.

'Hold up,' said Ramone. 'I thought y'all wuz from Mississippi. Y'all best not be fixin' to mess with Julius Ramone.'

'Mr Ramone, I can only apologise. There must have been some kind of misunderstanding. My business partner and I are from the United Kingdom,' said LeCarre.

'The United Kingdom, huh? I like dat. Well, dis be ma mothercrappin' Kingdom. What y'all want with a mother-crapper like me? My girl said y'all wanted to talk. So let's talk. Like we three mothercrappers recordin' a mothercrappin' podcast for BBC Sounds.'

'My associate and I have a business proposition.'

'Business proposition, huh? What is dis? The popular British television programme *Dragon's Den*?' said Julius Ramone. 'If that be da case then "I'm out". I love yo country, shit like *Fawlty Towers* got me and all my homies howlin' our damn asses off but I don't do no business with no strangers – y'all dig?'

'I dig,' said LeCarre. 'It's a shame. My client in Exeter was very interested in your product.'

LeCarre could sense Rhodes searching his Leicester De Montfort-educated mind for where he was going. Roger had made a calculation. If Sebastian Twine's visit to New York had some connection with the drugs trade and Julius Ramone then the mention of 'Exeter' could prise a reaction from Ramone.

'Exeter, huh?' Ramone raised one of his pierced eye-brows. 'Three hundred and fifteen feet! Ain't Exeter Cathedral got the longest uninterrupted vaulted ceiling in England? Three hundred and fifteen feet! That's a damn long mothercrappin' vaulted ceiling!'

The first thing everyone said at the mention of Exeter. New York had the Statue of Liberty, Paris had the Eiffel Tower and Exeter had the longest uninterrupted vaulted ceiling in England. LeCarre studied Ramone. He'd merely stated a fact everyone on earth knew. Beyond that Exeter didn't seem to arouse a flicker. LeCarre had hoped that Julius Ramone would give them an explanation for the deaths of Twine and Fade, just let the facts of the case fall from his mouth like a KitKat Chunky from a vending machine. If Ramone had said that he knew someone from Exeter, that he'd met someone from Exeter just a couple of weeks before – Sebastian Twine – and that Sebastian Twine had helped to arrange a drug deal between Ramone and Donkey Malone, and that he'd heard that Malone had since murdered Twine and another associate by the name of Charlie Fade for some reason which Ramone would neatly explain in the telling – well, that would be nice, but police work wasn't nice. Police work wasn't easy. Police work was tough. As tough as the crocodile leather on which they sat.

So why *did* Twine visit New York? LeCarre thought of Occam's razor, the philosophical principle that the most logical explanation, the one that requires the fewest assumptions, is usually the correct one.

Twine had simply visited New York to buy something from the Edinburgh Woollen Mill. That was the only explanation for which they had any evidence.

LeCarre wasn't thinking straight. Carrie and LeBron's affair mixed with the energy tariff situation had addled his mind and he'd concocted a series of wild theories and dragged Rhodes across the Atlantic on a wild-goose chase. The answer to who killed Charlie Fade and Sebastian Twine was in Exeter and yet here they were, 3,335 miles away in a Harlem nightclub.

'Well, Mr Ramone. If you're not interested in making a deal then I've taken up too much of your time,' LeCarre said to the New York drug lord.

'Hold up. You two mothercrappers ain't leavin' my mothercrappin' office until my hospitable ass offers you a mothercrappin' hit.'

A hit?

*Drugs.*

LeCarre clenched his fist. The bass from the nightclub reverberated through the soles of his brown brogues as he watched Julius Ramone present a silver tray on which sat a small mountain of white powder.

*Drugs. Illegal drugs.*

Rhodes, who was still there even though he hasn't been mentioned for quite a while, tried to disguise his gulp and assess the situation. This was enough drugs to send Julius Ramone down for a very long time, which is a police term for going to prison. Detective Mac Mullally had gone home – they were on their own – two fish out of water on the other side of the pond. This wasn't their jurisdiction. Did they even have the right to make an arrest? And if they did, the risks were as high as the people on the dance floor. Who knew what weapons Ramone had behind his alligator-shaped desk? Or how many henchmen were just behind the door? By the time Rhodes had come to the conclusion that the only sensible option was to make their excuses and leave, LeCarre had a Glock 19 pointed at Julius Ramone's heavily tattooed face.

'Put the drugs down and your hands up. Devon and Cornwall Police.'

Detective Roger LeCarre wasn't a man who made such assessments. The world was a simple place to him. He saw a drink – he drank it. He saw a KitKat Chunky – he ate it. He saw a crime – he made a goddamn arrest. No matter the circumstances.

LeCarre and Ramone stared into each other's eyes, each man looking for weakness, neither finding it. This wasn't the first time Julius Ramone had had a gun in his face and this wasn't the first time Detective Roger LeCarre had looked into the face of evil.

'*Put the drugs down and your hands up.*'

'Just my luck. I try and be nice to y'all and y'all try and arrest my ass,' said Ramone. 'I feel like a hapless character in one of yo hilarious mothercrappin' British sitcoms.'

'Just do as I say, Julius, and you won't get hurt.'

'You know, it's funny ... ' Julius was still holding the silver tray of drugs. 'Here we are. Chattin' away like my ass is Graham Norton and y'all a couple of guests on my mothercrappin' couch and I don't even know yo names.'

'This is Detective Tim Rhodes and my name is Detective Roger LeCarre.'

'Detective Roger LeCarre, huh? Well, it's a pleasure to meet yo ass, Detective Roger LeCarre. I like to know a mothercrapper's name before I pop a mothercrappin cap in his mothercrappin ass ... '

It all happened in less than a second.

The tray flying into the air. The alligator-shaped desk flipping over. Ramone picking up two Uzis and pointing them directly at LeCarre and Rhodes.

BANG. BANG. BANG. BANG. BANG.

Two in the chest. Two in the head. One just between the lower intestine and the urinary bladder.

He flew across the room and hit the wall behind him.

*Dead.*

Roger LeCarre took a few steps and stood over Julius Ramone because, just to be clear, Ramone was the one who got shot and LeCarre was the one who shot him.

'That was for Princess Di.'

'What?' said Rhodes.

'Sorry. I've never shot anyone before. I always fantasised about saying that when I did but now I realise in the moment that it's completely inappropriate.'

They both looked at Julius Ramone, hunched against the wall. Blood still poured from his body like water flowing through the River Exe. The python hissed and made its way up the wall and over the gallery of framed photographs. Pictures of better times at Stallion. Pictures of parties and dancing and drug-induced joy. Pictures of criminals, no doubt, but captured as they were they just looked like people.

One face stood out. A young man, arm in arm with Julius Ramone, a huge smile on his face.

*Sebastian Twine.*

# TWENTY

The five-foot-two flight attendant stepped out of the shower and slipped into a dressing gown. Her waist was 24 inches, her salary £24,000. The symmetry was pleasing, but she'd have preferred it if her salary aligned with her 42-inch bosom, giving her a salary of £42,000 per annum – not a spectacular sum, but comfortably above the national average of £29,600 before tax.

Detective Roger LeCarre watched her from the bed. His own stats were changing – from a flaccid three inches to a more impressive eight. Eight thousand pounds would be a terrible salary, but for an erect penis, eight inches was something to be relatively proud of. Certainly above average, especially given that most men tended to overstate their size when surveyed.

Detective LeCarre surveyed the young woman's body,

just like she'd hoped that a chartered surveyor would one day survey a property for her should her salary ever get closer to aligning with her chest size rather than her waist which is to say over £40,000 although realistically that wouldn't be enough for a mortgage on her own.

*She wasn't on her own now.*

She was with Detective Roger LeCarre whose salary was considerably larger than his waist size but could be about to shrink to nothing if Chief Superintendent Beverley Chang ever found out what had happened in New York just a matter of hours earlier.

Roger LeCarre was supposed to doing things by The Book but he'd flown to New York and shot and killed the most notorious criminal on the East Coast of America. In a just world he would be receiving a 'thank you' phone call from the president of the United States, maybe a ticker tape parade, but LeCarre didn't live in a just world. Anyone who'd seen the way energy bills had risen over the last few years knew that.

They'd had to decide what to do quick. Ramone's ragged crew would be out for revenge. America wasn't safe for LeCarre any more. He was the triggerman. He had to get out of town.

Out of the frying pan and into the fire.

Exeter.

Now they knew for sure that Twine had been associating with Julius Ramone they had to follow that lead, so Rhodes stayed in New York to investigate. Perhaps he would get to see *Death of a Salesman* starring Marisa Tomei after all.

LeCarre and Rhodes had argued before his flight back.

'I can't believe you let us get into such a dangerous situation,' Rhodes had said. 'I'm about to become a father. If I hang around you much longer the young men in my antenatal class will have a higher death rate than the young men in the First World War.'

'That's a cumbersome analogy,' LeCarre had said.

'You don't know your own power, LeCarre.'

Maybe it was best they had some time away from each other. Lately, everything LeCarre touched seemed to fall apart. Everything except the beautiful British Airways flight attendant he was currently making love to.

They had sex three more incredible times and one more fair-to-middling time because Roger was getting tired, then she slid back into her uniform and kissed him goodbye at the door.

'Next time your flight schedule takes you to Exeter, be sure to let me know,' said LeCarre.

'Actually, I usually fly out of Gatwick so I doubt I'll be down this way again,' the nameless woman said.

'Oh right, in that case then, bye.'

'OK, bye!'

And suddenly, like Julius Ramone, she was gone and out of his life except not because he'd shot her but because, as she'd just said, her schedule didn't usually take her to Exeter.

LeCarre was alone again. Alone with his complex thoughts. He poured himself a glass of recently purchased duty-free whisky, sat back in his ergonomic leather chair, picked up a pad and a Parker pen which he'd acquired a few months ago for inquiring about life insurance, and started to make some notes.

Sebastian Twine – according to Mayor Rufus Scallion, his boss, Twine had been associating with Donkey Malone. He now knew he'd been associating with the previously living Julius Ramone, too. Was Twine helping to arrange some kind of deal between Ramone and Malone? Were the great criminal dynasties of America and Devon joining forces? This could be like when Kraft bought Cadbury's. It seemed odd that Twine, a council worker, could have risen so quickly in Malone's ranks that he'd been entrusted with such a job. Or maybe Twine was acting alone? That would have angered Malone. Or Twine had made some kind of faux pas on American soil, like saying 'pavement' instead of 'sidewalk', and Ramone sent a hitman to Exeter to take him out? So many possibilities and, yet, so few certainties. The whole case was like watching a particularly tough round on *Only Connect* with Victoria Coren-Mitchell.

Charlie Fade – none of the theories for Twine's murder seemed to explain Charlie Fade's. But Twine had wanted to tell LeCarre something about Fade's murder so there had to be a connection.

Beverley Chang – she was up to something. Telling LeCarre to stay away from Malone was like telling him to stay away from the offer of a free Parker pen – you couldn't. Then there were the payments into her account from DM Enterprises. She may not have carried out the deed but LeCarre definitely had reason to be suspicious she could be covering for Malone.

Rufus Scallion – was the charismatic roly-poly mayor being straight with them? According to his story he suspected Sebastian Twine, one of his staff, was taking drugs and mixing with Donkey Malone's crew and yet he didn't think to mention it to the police until Twine was dead. All politicians lie. Did they murder, too?

Donkey Malone – LeCarre underlined his name again

and again. All roads led to Donkey Malone. But LeCarre had zero evidence. If he wanted to put Malone in a box (prison) then LeCarre had to think *outside* the box. What if he came up with a mnemonic for his name? Could that help? He started to write.

Dangerous
'Orrible
Naughty
Kriminal
Evil
Young at heart

Murderer
Angry
Launderer?
Odd
Negligent
Exasperating

LeCarre stared at the words on the pad. Surely there must be something there that could help to crack the case. There had to be. He tried underlining each word, then circling them, then drawing little arrows towards them. Nothing.

It was clear LeCarre wasn't going to solve the case from the comfort of his lever-operated ergonomic chair with adjustable arms. He had to follow his nose and right now his nose was pointed towards Donkey Malone. It didn't matter what Chang had said. Roger LeCarre was a renegade cop and renegade cops didn't listen to their superiors: they listened to their guts. It was time to go back to the ghetto.

# TWENTY-ONE

A slow-moving tornado made its way through the Skibblemead Estate, a tornado in leather jacket and brown brogues, a tornado in search of a killer. The tornado was whistling and carrying a baseball bat it had bought as a souvenir from New York. A tornado can rip apart a house in seconds, but tornados don't usually know where they're going. This one did.

Detective Roger LeCarre, who was the tornado, by the way, smashed down Donkey Malone's front door.

Tina, Donkey's hoop-earringed girlfriend, screamed. Behind her stood an unfazed Donkey Malone, in boxers and a silk dressing gown, a cigar in his criminal mouth.

'Detective LeCarre,' he said, calmly. 'You could have told me you were coming. I'd have baked a cake.'

'I'm on a diet. Time to talk Twine, Donkey,' said

LeCarre, smashing his bat against the wall. 'Sebastian Twine.'

'Take a seat, Detective, and put that bat down or I'll call Chang. You wanna be careful – another disciplinary incident and you'll be hearing from HR.'

LeCarre thought about shattering Malone's glass coffee table but decided against it on the grounds that Tina would probably unfairly be the one who'd have to clean up the mess. It could be overdoing it. Malone was the criminal and yet LeCarre was the one waving a baseball bat around like a madman. The lines were getting blurred.

LeCarre sat down, resting the bat beside him, ready to swing it again should the need arise.

'Twine. Tell me about Twine,' said LeCarre.

'Who?' said Malone.

*'Sebastian Twine.'*

*'I don't know who you're talking about,'* said Malone, proving LeCarre wasn't the only one who could talk in italics.

'Let me give you a little biography,' said LeCarre. 'Sebastian Twine was a young man with a bright future at Exeter City Council. He had a baby on the way and a skip in his step. Then he started getting into indie music and art and spoken-word poetry, which all led to drugs, and when you start taking drugs in this town, that leads to you.'

'Stop it, Detective, you're making me blush,' said Malone, sarcastically, because he wasn't blushing, he was puffing on his cigar.

'When you came across Twine you realised that having a smart young man on your side, instead of the idiots you usually surround yourself with, could be useful. Especially one who came with the legitimacy of being an employee of Mayor Rufus Scallion. So you sent Twine to New York to negotiate a deal with Julius Ramone to bring the new drug Dalliance to Exeter. He'd successfully negotiated the contract for the new pelican crossing on Priory Road so why not an international drugs deal, huh? He was happy for the free trip and the opportunity to visit the new branch of Edinburgh Woollen Mill in Times Square – and of course to taste a hot new drug. But soon after his return you killed Charlie Fade, for being a mouthy kid, and Twine realised it didn't feel good to be on the same team as a murderer. So Twine called me to spill the beans but you don't like spilled beans, spilled beans are difficult to clean up, so you killed Twine and now you've killed two people in one week and you've taken to walking around your house in a dressing gown wondering when you'll be getting your next visit from Detective Roger LeCarre, Well, here I am, Donkey. Here I am.'

Donkey clapped slowly in that way that villains in movies do.

'Bravo, Detective! Bravo! You've cracked the case.' He pointed his wrists towards LeCarre. 'Well, come on then, handcuff me. Guess I'll be going away for a long, long time. There's only one problem. You're like a climate change scientist – you've got no evidence.'

'CCTV places you where Charlie Fade was found dead around the time of the murder.'

'Saturday night in Exeter city centre. Lot of people around if I remember right, Detective. Maybe I'd just been to see Josh Widdicombe's tour show. You don't have enough and you know it,' said Malone.

'Nice coffee table. I think I remember seeing it in John Lewis,' said LeCarre. 'You shop there often? Perhaps you were there on Monday? Pop into the café by any chance?'

'You're floundering. If you're Exeter's Person of the Year then we're in worse trouble than I thought.'

'Well, *you'll* be in even worse trouble than *you* thought when I catch you,' said LeCarre, wishing he could think of a better line.

Donkey Malone leaned in for emphasis. 'I like you, LeCarre. You're a worthy opponent and I hate to see you off your game, so I'm going to throw you a bone.'

LeCarre hated the position he was in but he wanted that bone more than anything. He opened his ears as wide as he could.

'You're asking the wrong questions, Roger LeCarre, and you're sniffing around the wrong places. If I was you I'd be worried about what's going on closer to home. A hundred and twenty-two Quaverly Street. That's where the answer to the question you *should* be asking is.'

# TWENTY-TWO

The question he *should* be asking? What was that? What do a.m. and p.m. stand for? Where do raisins come from? What happened to Dido? She was everywhere and then suddenly she was nowhere. Was Dido at 122 Quaverly Street? Was that why Donkey had sent him there? To find Dido?

He'd have his answer soon.

Quaverly Street was just a few yards from Malone's flat, deep in the heart of the ghetto, in the belly of the beast. The average house price in Exeter was just over £300,000. In Quaverly Street? You'd be lucky to get £160,000, even with a new kitchen fitted, so that gives you some idea of the depravation.

LeCarre stood on the pavement in front of number 122. The overgrown grass in the front garden failed to conceal six discarded shopping trolleys and two washing machines. It was hard to believe that some people lived like this. It had all the signs of being a crack den. Or a Gasmask den. Whatever it was, it was a den of drugs, a den of misery.

LeCarre knocked on the door.

He waited.

And waited.

Then knocked again.

Eventually a young man, an apparent junkie, answered.

'Wot?'

'Detective Roger LeCarre. Devon and Cornwall Police.'

LeCarre could have swept the place, called for backup, put some junkies in a van and called it a productive day, but that wasn't why he was there. He was there looking for the answer to a question he didn't know yet. He made a quick note in his mind – that could be a good quiz show format worth attempting to sell to a London TV company.

So mangled by drugs was the junkie's mind that he let LeCarre in without even thinking about it. It wasn't Detective Roger LeCarre's first visit to a drug hovel and it probably wouldn't be his last. All the usual paraphernalia was there: fags, reggae music, a floor that didn't look like it had been hoovered in days. A washing machine bleeped, signalling the end of its cycle. Not one of the drug fiends thought to get up and put the laundry on a clothes horse.

They just sat there, mindlessly staring into space. Did they even give the washing machine its recommended once-a-month empty cycle with a cup of hot vinegar? Was the washing machine even under warranty? Or had they spent that money on drugs too? Drugs have a way of making a human give up on life.

LeCarre walked from room to room, disgusted at everything he saw. Unwashed tea mugs, disorganised bookshelves, a colour scheme that simply *did not work*. It was hard to believe that some people lived like this. They were beyond help, that's the way LeCarre saw it. Some called addiction a disease, something we should have sympathy for. LeCarre saw it as a choice – a choice to live off the grid, to ignore the responsibilities of being a citizen. These were the kind of people who didn't watch the Queen's speech on Christmas Day, watched a film instead, probably opened their Christmas crackers and stuck the hats on their heads without even bothering to read out the jokes – the scum of the earth.

Lock them all up and throw away the key. Not that that would do any good, now that prisons were six-star hotels with triple-Michelin-starred food and marble water features. Given the choice between a week in St Lucia and a six-month stretch in a luxury slammer, LeCarre would probably take the latter. Arresting them wasn't worth the paperwork.

Today was about something else – he just didn't know what that something else was yet.

LeCarre made it to the kitchen-diner. A breakfast table had two-day-old newspapers strewn across it, discarded relics of a time before the latest binge.

A packet of white powder. A packet of *drugs*. LeCarre picked it up and put it in his pocket. One small dent in the drug mountain that towered over Exeter. He'd get it tested. Could be cocaine, could be something else, could be Gasmask. Whatever it was, it was unlikely to be Calgon washing machine cleaner.

He walked up the badly carpeted stairs and looked in each of the bedrooms: unmade beds, posters of marijuana leaves, poorly put-together flat-pack furniture – your classic crack den.

And then he saw it, the most shocking thing he'd seen in twenty-four years on the Devon and Cornwall police force: a fourteen-year-old girl injecting a Gasmask pipe into her veins.

'Hey there, kiddo. Why don't you put the drugs down and come over here? You like mints? I've got a packet of Extra Strong in my pocket.'

But then the girl looked up and suddenly LeCarre knew

that it was he and not the mints that would have to be extra strong, and not in a taste sense but in an emotional sense, because the junkie girl . . . *was his daughter.*

Destiny LeCarre. Roger's little angel. The day she was born, which was sometime in June or maybe July, was the most incredible day of his life. He'd vowed always to take care of her.

'I will always take care of you,' he'd said to her even though at just a few hours old, she'd had next to no comprehension of the English language.

But he hadn't taken care of her. He'd been so focused on saving Devon and Cornwall from crime (and also his pub quiz team) that he'd neglected to save *her* from crime. He'd failed as a father. Destiny's destiny wasn't supposed to be this. Fourteen years of age and on her way to a rehab facility. Whenever LeCarre was out on the streets and saw a child committing crime or taking drugs, he'd asked, 'Where are the parents?' It turns out this particular parent was out on the streets asking, 'Where are the parents?'

Donkey Malone was right. LeCarre wasn't asking the right questions. He should have been asking where his daughter was. The truth was the answer to that question was too tough to bear.

# TWENTY-THREE

Back in central Exeter, back where it all started, five minutes' walk from where Charlie Fade was found dead and just a few yards from the construction of Rufus Scallion's soon-to-be-unveiled Ferris wheel. That hadn't started turning yet but Detective Roger LeCarre's mind had – *a Ferris wheel of thoughts.*

He had chosen neutral territory. This time he wasn't meeting a criminal, not unless sleeping with your husband's partner is a crime.

He was meeting Carrie.

The famous central Exeter breeze caressed his rugged face. In the three days since he'd last seen his wife, Roger had slept with three women, witnessed the death of Sebastian Twine, been to New York, killed the most notorious crime boss on the East Coast of America and had his first cappuccino. They sure had a lot of catching up to do.

But they weren't there to talk about cappuccino. They were there to talk about Destiny.

*Their daughter.*

Roger had made a decision. No matter how he felt about Carrie and her betrayal, no matter how difficult it was for him, the most important thing was to be civil. This wasn't about Roger and Carrie – it was about Destiny. They had to put any personal grudges aside and decide together what was best for their daughter.

Carrie arrived.

'You're two minutes late,' said LeCarre. 'Fucking LeBron, I suppose? Nice dress. Who bought it for you? Was it LeBron? *My old partner*?'

'Roger . . . '

'Oh, you've remembered my name, have you? Remembered any other names? Maybe LEBRON? Ring any bells? You know . . . LeBron Jax! Used to be my partner but then you *fucked him*?'

Carrie wasn't used to hearing Roger swear. The only time she could think of was a brief period when he got especially into singing along to 'Living Next Door to Alice'

187

featuring Roy Chubby Brown in the car. That was good-natured, hilarious swearing. This wasn't.

'Roger, please, let me speak,' said Carrie. 'I'm sorry. I'm sorry for the hurt I caused you.'

'Pah!'

Roger turned his back to Carrie, hiding the tears in his eyes. Across the street was a Betfred. What odds would he get on he and Carrie getting back together? Probably a 100 billion to one.

He felt a hand on his shoulder. It was a familiar hand, a beautiful hand, a hand he still loved. It was Carrie's left hand.

'I just don't understand,' said Roger, his back still turned. 'Why did you do it, Carrie? I know I wasn't perfect. I know I said I'd get us on a new energy tariff but ... *this case* ... I've still got until the end of the week before the new rate kicks in. Was it the housework? Look, I know you do all the cleaning but I always take the bins out and I think you don't really seem to even see that as a job, you never give me any credit for it. I'm not saying it's as much work as all the cleaning but it's still hard work and me not doing the cleaning is no reason to have an affair with LeBron. Plus I wash the car so—'

'Roger, that's not why I slept with LeBron.'

Roger spun back around to face Carrie, completing his 360-degree turn.

'Then why?' he pleaded. Roger LeCarre wasn't a man who pled but here he was in central Exeter pleading before his adulterous wife for all the world to see. '*Why*?'

A single tear rose up through Carrie's body, fell out of her eye and landed on the concrete between them. Splash. The sound of it hitting the ground was impossible to ignore. It told Roger that he wasn't the only one who was hurt.

'We're not here to talk about us, Roger,' said Carrie. 'We're here to talk about Destiny.'

A fourteen-year-old in a drug den, mashed up on Gasmask. How could they let it happen? Too much screen time? Was that it? She'd been listening to a lot of K-Pop. Were there hidden messages in the songs? The city's drug scene was a whirlpool, dragging the citizens down. Maybe the younger you were, the harder it was to resist its pull. Scallion was right. They needed this Ferris wheel more than anything. The youth needed to set their sights towards a brighter future, not the gutter. A big Ferris wheel could do that.

*It just made sense.*

Roger ran his hand through his jet-black hair like he was searching for answers; all he found was the texture and thickness of a much younger man.

'She's in good care. The doctors will know what to do,'

he said, desperately wanting to believe his own words. 'Maybe it's good for her to get her crisis in young. This time next year this will all be a distant memory and she can be a little girl again, doing all the things little girls love to do – skipping, drawing unicorns, helping their dad train for pub quizzes.'

Carrie breathed deeply into her chest, making her breasts look a little larger. 'I never stopped loving you, you know, Roger.'

'Then why, Carrie? *Why?*'

'Your work. You were always so fixated with your damn work,' said Carrie. 'There was always a case that seemed to take up all of your attention. There wasn't enough time for us.'

'Carrie . . . this city . . . '

'I know, Roger. This city needs you.' She began to sob in a way that would look really good in a film. 'But I needed you too.'

Then Roger asked the question he never wanted to ask. Even more than 'Can you repeat question seven, please?' because if you ask a quizmaster to repeat a question you are essentially accusing them of not being clear enough in the first place.

'Don't you need me any more, Carrie?'

'Don't ... I can't do this. I knew about all the other women, Roger.'

Roger couldn't believe she was bringing up his roughly eighty to 120 infidelities. That seemed like a low blow. His erotic escapades were a simple means of keeping himself focused. If a man, a real man like Roger LeCarre, doesn't tend that particular garden then he can't think of anything else. It's just a biological fact that men need casual sex with a range of beautiful women to be good at their jobs. It was nothing like what Carrie had done.

Carrie fixed him with her hazel gaze.

'You were hardly *semper fidelis*, Roger.'

*Semper fidelis*! That phrase again! The one that was carved into both of the bodies. Do you remember? *Semper fidelis*. Rhodes had found out what it meant – 'always faithful'.

How did Carrie know that phrase? She didn't speak Latin, not as far as Roger knew. He'd never asked. Carrie had been there the night that Charlie Fade had been killed. It couldn't ... she couldn't ...

'*Semper fidelis*,' said Roger. 'How do you know that phrase?'

'What do you mean how do I know it?'

Roger took a step closer. Suddenly he was a police officer again.

'*How do you know that phrase, Ms LeCarre?*'

'Roger . . . '

'Detective Roger LeCarre, madam.'

'Roger, every Exonian knows that phrase. It's our city motto.'

How could Roger not know? He cursed himself, but then he hadn't grown up in Exeter, he was a child of Totnes. It had just passed him by. Rhodes was from out of town, too. '*Semper fidelis*' had escaped them both. LeCarre thought back to all the letters he'd received from the council when he was campaigning to save Exeter's best-loved zebra crossing. The letterhead had featured Exeter's coat of arms. He could see it in his mind now: a pair of winged horses, the castle and two words – *semper fidelis*. Of course.

The cogs in LeCarre's Ferris wheel-sized brain were turning. Some things you couldn't see from up close. Crop circles, for example. Crop circles were best viewed from above. Now LeCarre was rising high above this case in his mind-helicopter and looking down on it. He was starting to see the whole picture. It was beautiful. But he couldn't be sure. The image was still blurred.

*Someone else was looking down from above, not metaphorically, but literally. Looking down on Roger and Carrie LeCarre. Their eyes narrowed.*

Roger and Carrie's eyes weren't narrowing – they were open wide and directed at each other. She'd told him she still loved him. Maybe the odds weren't a billion to one. If he walked into Betfred now he'd be lucky to get 5/4.

'I have to go. I think I might be about to crack this case. There's something I need to do.'

Carrie understood but she had to ask. 'And Destiny?'

'I'll set up a direct debit for the rehab. She'll be fine.'

'Thank you, Roger.'

Roger paused for one brief second and looked at her, Carrie LeCarre. With the exception of Myleene Klass, she was still the most beautiful woman he had ever seen.

Roger always knew that the ravages of time might change that fact but he didn't expect it to happen in a second.

*But then . . .*

Suddenly her beauty dropped by 8,000 per cent. 8,000 per cent? Seems like a lot, doesn't it? But that's what a sniper's bullet can do to a head.

Roger didn't see the bullet hit his wife but he saw what it did. He saw the *puff* upon impact. He saw her hit the ground like she'd just been shot.

*Because she had.*

He saw the blood make its way towards his brown

193

brogues and he didn't even care. Obviously he cared about the fact that his wife had just been shot but he didn't care about the blood on his shoes . . .

*Because his wife had just been shot.*

# TWENTY-FOUR

*Bleep, bleep, bleep, bleep . . .*

The bleeps were messing with Detective Roger LeCarre's mind but he didn't want them to stop because that would mean his wife was dead. The bleeps were the only thing keeping her alive. Or at least that's the way he thought it worked – he hadn't really been listening when the doctor had spoken. LeCarre felt like a bullet had gone through *his* brain.

This was turning out to be the most eventful week since the London Olympics.

Roger could hardly bring himself to look at Carrie's face. Even if he wanted to it would be impossible, covered as it was in bandages. Was it even Carrie underneath that mountain of dressings? Yes. Somehow, her unmistakable aura found its way through, and also the Glow by Jennifer Lopez perfume he'd given her for her birthday. It wasn't her shocking appearance that made LeCarre want to turn away. It was the shame.

He hadn't protected her or Destiny. He hadn't protected them and he hadn't protected the city. He had failed as a detective and as a man.

Eighty to 120 infidelities. She was right. How could he do that to his wife? That was far too many. A few slip-ups were inevitable but any more than thirty was just wrong. Roger LeCarre was changing, changing like a protagonist in a really well-plotted novel. All it had taken for him to do so was the destruction of his wife and daughter.

He placed his hand on that beautiful left hand of hers. LeCarre was trembling. There was only so much one man could take. The weight of the world was on his shoulders, which according to the internet is 5.9 trillion trillion kilograms. That was a lot of weight, thought LeCarre, before pondering how they had gone about weighing it.

He'd thought he'd solved the case but why would they want to kill Carrie? LeCarre walked over to the hospital window in an attempt to look meaningfully over the city but all he could actually see was the car park. Somewhere out there was the killer, or maybe the killer's car. LeCarre *had* to find them and smother them with justice but he was in no fit state. His nerves were severely jangled.

LeCarre hunched over, a defeated man, hands in pockets. His hands could feel all the usual things – phone, keys, badge, debit card, RAC card, squash club card, Extra Strong mints – but there was something unfamiliar, too. He took it out and looked at it.

The packet of white powder from 122 Quaverly Street, the packet of *drugs*.

LeCarre was shaking; he was a mess. He needed to get it together. Dammit, he needed to feel something other than the pain pumping through his West Country heart. Maybe this packet of drugs was the solution. Just the once?

One LeCarre fist was clenched, stubbornly sticking to his usual anti-drugs stance, the other hand was frantically chopping the substance up with a Devon & Exeter Squash Club membership card on the end of his wife's hospital bed.

*Just the once.*

He took a straw from Carrie's bedside table. She wouldn't be using it any time soon. To all intents and purposes she didn't have a mouth.

A thousand tiny crystals shot up Detective Roger LeCarre's nose and straight into his brain. No going back now.

*Bleep, bleep, bleep, bleep . . .*

Something inside LeCarre moved. It sounded like a beat. Before he knew it Roger LeCarre was dancing in his wife's hospital room to sound of her life-support machine and it was the best music he had ever heard.

*Bleep, bleep, bleep, bleep . . .*

Roger LeCarre's limbs were making rapid shapes. He'd seen those moves so many times before, made by wild-eyed hedonists, just before he pulled them out of a Bodmin rave and threw them into the back of a police van. Now he was one of them and it felt amazing.

He was supposed to be hunting a killer but all his body wanted to do was hunt the rhythm, stay here, looking up at the fluorescent hospital lights, dancing to his wife's struggling heartbeat.

Just a few more minutes.

No.

NO!

Detective Roger LeCarre powered through the double doors and out into the hospital corridor, letting out the animal cry of a man who'd just ingested illegal drugs for the first time.

'Arrrrghhhh!'

He looked down at his Fitbit – 240 beats per minute. Was that normal? It seemed like a lot. Still carefully following hospital guidelines and washing his hands, he caught a glimpse of himself in the mirror. Eyes the size of avocado stones, sweat pouring down his face like fat down a recently basted turkey. He didn't look well.

Through another set of doors and into the hospital waiting room. Was he hallucinating like some kind of drug man? Detective Superintendent Beverley Chang was standing beside his former friend LeBron Jax.

'Did I miss something? Whose birthday is it?' LeCarre's words exited his mouth like slurred droplets of fury. He wanted to sound sober. He didn't.

'Roger, I'm so sorry. We wanted to be here for you and Carrie,' said Chang.

'Give me some space, Chang,' said LeCarre, as he made his way over to the vending machine in search of a KitKat Chunky. 'Damn it, has anyone got any change?'

'Roger. Are you sure you're OK?'

'I'm fine, Jax! I'm fine! One pound twenty? These would be no more than 80p in a shop! This is what's wrong with the bloody NHS! No wonder it's on its knees!'

'You don't look fine, Roger,' said Jax.

'Let me look at your eyes,' said Chang, assessing the ragged man in front of her. 'Roger, have you just taken Gasmask?'

'What? No! Jet lagged! I'm just jet lagged!'

'Here,' said Chang, handing him some change. 'Get yourself something to eat, go home and get some rest.'

'I don't want your dirty money, Chang! I know where you got it from.'

DM Enterprises. Those extra payments into her account. He may have seen it in the throes of sexual ecstasy, but he remembered.

'Roger, what in the heck are you talking about?' said Chang.

'Take it easy, buddy,' said LeBron.

'Back off! I'm not your buddy, buddy,' said LeCarre, cleverly saying the word buddy twice in a way that sounded cool.

'Seriously, Roger. I think you need to go home,' said Chang. 'We'll look out for Carrie. We'll let you know if there's any news.'

'Oh, you'll look out for her, will you?' panted LeCarre. 'How are you going to do that? Whoever shot Carrie is still out there. Heck, Chang, maybe they're in this room. Maybe I'm looking right at them. Maybe you did it,' he said, before manically banging on the vending machine and hoping a KitKat Chunky would fall out, just like he'd fallen out of love with his city. LeCarre's Fitbit buzzed, congratulating him on breaking a new record – 5,000 calories burnt in the last ten minutes.

'Give me your badge, Roger,' said Chang. 'You're not working this case any more. I'm suspending you.'

'What do you mean I'm not working this case? I want the finest detective west of Taunton searching for the killer and that just so happens to be me.'

'I'm afraid there's one problem.'

'Oh yeah? What's that? Diversity quotas? You telling me I gotta step aside for a woman in a wheelchair again?'

'No, this time it's a different problem to the one you just said. This time the problem is that you're clearly high on illegal drugs which, as you and I both know ... *is a crime.*'

# TWENTY-FIVE

Detective Roger LeCarre picked up another stone and threw it into the River Exe. He'd *come down* to the river on his *comedown*. He was *throwing rocks* and he was at *rock bottom*. Sometimes it was impossible not to see the beautiful poetry that ran through life, like this river ran through Devon and also a little bit of Somerset.

He'd never felt so low. Not even when he'd visited the King Edward Mine Museum in Camborne and actually taken a tour underground with his now coma-ridden wife and that went 400 feet below sea level. Roger LeCarre was a copper, a copper to his core. If you cut him open he'd bleed blue and handcuffs and truncheons and stuff would come out. Right now he was a copper without a badge and there was nothing worse than a copper without a badge. It was like a tortoise without a shell, a vacuum cleaner without a bag, a combi boiler without a five-year warranty.

'Life!' he exclaimed, to no one but himself.

What a thing it was. How could God let all this happen? If there was a God. LeCarre wasn't sure any more. Maybe there was just an energy that we called God or maybe we were all just characters in a video game being played by aliens on a more advanced planet in another galaxy or maybe the Hindus were right and there was a big elephant man with loads of arms or something – is that what they thought?

Whoever or whatever it was that controlled events, it wasn't on Detective Roger LeCarre's side right now, that was for sure. He looked up at the grey sky. Exeter's natural ceiling was no Sistine Chapel. It looked grim and foreboding and also like it might rain in a bit.

LeCarre skimmed another stone. Just three jumps. Even his throwing was off. A bird perched for a moment on a small cluster of rocks at the other side of the water. If only I could be that bird and fly away from here and leave all my troubles, thought LeCarre, completely originally.

The bird made its way over to LeCarre's side of the river and perched beside him. A friend? He sure needed one. Roger felt so alone. Time catches up with every man eventually. Was this LeCarre's time? That goal of his – to rid the world of crime. It wasn't going very well. Two murders, a shot wife – and even *he* had taken drugs. Things had got so bad in Exeter that Detective Roger LeCarre was breaking the law.

Perhaps it was time, for the first time in his life, to give up. He had a half-decent pension. Why not cash it in, move to St Ives, join the painting community? He'd never actually sat down and painted before but it couldn't be that hard. Have you seen some of the rubbish they call art these days?

The bird was pecking at something, a small ridge in the riverbank. Each peck produced a metallic sound, reminding LeCarre of the time he and Carrie went to Plymouth to see a touring production of the percussive musical extravaganza *Stomp*. Would they ever do such a thing again? Would they ever go to Zizzi's again? Would they ever visit the South Devon Railway again? Or Bicton Park Botanical Gardens? Or Woodlands Family Theme Park? Or any of the other top Devon tourist attractions listed on TripAdvisor? In that moment, LeCarre made a vow to himself: if Carrie lived, he had to try and patch things up with her. Their marriage wasn't like the stone in his hand – he couldn't just throw it away.

That metallic pecking sound – what had the bird found?

LeCarre took two steps closer. Had he taken a third, he may have regretted it. Another man may not have known what it was he was looking at. Luckily, for Exeter, Detective Roger LeCarre had seen more than eight hundred hours of Nazi documentaries.

*A World War Two bomb.*

'Stand back! Clear the area!' LeCarre yelled at absolutely no one.

# TWENTY-SIX

'Roger, the bomb disposal team are here,' shouted Chief Superintendent Beverley Chang from the perimeter. 'They can send in the robot now.'

'Tell them to go home, Chang!' LeCarre replied. 'I'm doing this myself.'

Behind Chang were four hundred hastily evacuated houses. Had LeCarre eaten in the last twenty-four hours, he'd be hastily evacuating his bowels.

'Seriously, Roger. They're experts. This is their job, they do it all the time.'

'I'm defusing this bomb, Beverley,' said LeCarre. 'And some supposed experts in defusing bombs aren't going to stop me.'

LeCarre assessed the situation. Three inches of iron sticking out of the mud, three more metres of bomb nestling below the surface. It occurred to him that he had more in common with that unexploded World War Two bomb than any human. A lifetime of pent-up rage, hidden below a tough exterior. Now it was time to deal with it once and for all.

'Seriously, Roger,' said Chang, who was actually speaking to him through a radio now. 'Apparently it's very simple. They just send in the robot to carry out a controlled explosion. They've done it hundreds of times before. Trying to do it manually is an entirely unnecessary risk.'

'Beverley! No! I have to do this.'

*Life* was an unnecessary risk.

Detective Roger LeCarre had something to prove. If he could tame this World War Two bomb then maybe he could tame the destructive rage within his rotten soul, maybe he could tame this criminal bonfire of a city, this burning furnace of a world. Also, successfully starting and completing a task might give him the confidence to finally sort out his energy provider.

He'd already been suspended. If this went wrong he'd almost certainly lose his job, not that it mattered.

*Corpses don't have jobs.*

But if he got it right? Putting aside for a moment the fact that the bomb had lain dormant for eighty years and would have probably done so for another eight hundred, if he single-handedly saved the city from almost certain destruction, Chang would have to give him back his badge. Then he could put this case to bed and sort things out with Carrie and Destiny. Then he could rebuild his life.

'Right,' he said to himself, rubbing his hands together like he was about to tuck in to a delicious meal at Zizzi's. But this wasn't a delicious meal at Zizzi's.

*This was a bomb.*

LeCarre bent over and began to twist the cap off the top of the bomb because that's how bombs work. He thought of the time he twisted the cap off a bottle of Diet Coke in the station canteen and it exploded all over him. LeBron had shaken it up behind his back as a joke. Good times. If only that was the only thing LeBron had done behind his back.

The cap wasn't coming off easily.

'Rightie tightie, leftie loosey.'

Not loosey enough. Eighty years lodged into an Exeter riverbank can make things a little stiff.

Thank God LeCarre always carried lip balm. When Burt's Bees first created their signature Beeswax Lip Balm range, they probably never expected it to be applied to a Nazi instrument of war. 'Well, wake up Burt's Bees, Roger LeCarre has a city to save,' said Roger LeCarre.

He took the cap off his lip balm – a much easier job – and began to apply the lubricant to the tiny crack between the bomb cap and the rest of the device. He felt like his hand was shaking. This was the most nervous he'd been since The Enforcers had reached the final of the South-West Pub Quiz regionals and LeCarre was sent up to answer the tie-breaker. He'd won then. Could he win now? He reached into his leather jacket's inside pocket and took out his premium stainless-steel hip flask. Still some White Russian left. Although the cream was essentially cheese now, it was the vodka he needed. He took a sip, retched and went back to work.

The lip balm was working. LeCarre managed to get the bomb cap off and put it gently to one side. He took a look at the newly revealed bomb compartment. In front of him was a set of wires. I guess everyone has to defuse their first bomb sometime, thought LeCarre, picking up a nearby leaf and wiping the sweat from his brow.

He stopped for a moment. Savour it, he thought. It could be your last.

To his left was the Trews Weir Suspension Bridge. He'd stood and stared at that bridge so many times before, skimming stones, contemplating the complexities of this thing we call life. A pretty little structure, built for the people of

209

Exeter, helping them get to where they needed to go. To his right was the weir itself, a small dam, controlling the flow of the River Exe. Nature, tamed by man.

But man *was* nature. An unpredictable beast, vulnerable to base desires. Roger LeCarre himself was testament to that. Floods still happened. However much we try to control nature, sometimes it defeats us.

*Wait.*

LeCarre felt that familiar twitch. There it was. He'd been waiting for it ever since he first saw Charlie Fade's dead body. A flash of electrical current in his extraordinary brain. It happened every time.

He hadn't, had he?

He'd cracked the case!

He felt certain but then he'd felt certain before. At the end of 1999 he'd hidden in a cave on Dartmoor with six months' food supply in preparation for the Millennium Bug. He still remembered how he'd felt emerging in June 2000 and thinking, 'Oh, I probably didn't need to do that actually.'

No. This time the twitch was there. The twitch was never wrong. He just had to get the proof to send the killer down. Rhodes. He needed Rhodes. He'd call him as soon as he'd defused the bomb.

*The bomb!*

If LeCarre didn't defuse this bomb then he wouldn't be calling anyone and the killer would be free to continue their reign of terror.

What did LeCarre know about defusing bombs?

'Think, man! Think!'

From what he'd seen in films he'd have to cut a series of wires, taking care not to cut the wrong one. Cut the right wire – you disable the bomb. Cut the wrong one? Goodbye, Exeter. *That's how bombs work.* Having no wire cutters to hand he had two options: a) call Chang for help; or b) cut the wires with his teeth.

Teeth. It had to be teeth. After the humiliation of having his badge confiscated there was no way he could demean himself by asking for help.

Right. Which wire first?

'Eeny, meeny, miny, BANG!' he said to himself, like a cool character in an action film.

There were four wires. Red, yellow, blue and bitter-sweet shimmer.

'Come on, LeCarre, think like a Nazi,' he said to himself for the first time. 'Which colour would they deem dangerous?'

Red is traditionally the colour of danger, the wire to avoid. Think this through, though, he thought. This bomb was most likely made in 1940s Germany. Red was featured on the Nazi flag. Red is the colour of anger – a Nazi's favourite emotion. Red is the colour of blood – Nazis were obsessed with bloodlines. Nazis love red! The more he thought about it, red stood out as the least likely candidate. The red wire simply had to be the safe wire, the wire that defused the bomb.

Was he really going to do this? Bite into the red wire on a 1,000 kg bomb?

*Yes. Yes he was.*

Detective Roger LeCarre wasn't your ordinary man, your run-of-the-mill citizen. He was a man who knew what he wanted. He knew right from wrong, good from evil. He knew who'd killed Charlie Fade, he knew who'd killed Sebastian Twine and he knew that it was his duty to bite into this unexploded World War Two bomb.

So he did.

Years later people would always ask him what it tasted like, that red wire.

'Chicken,' he'd jokingly reply. The truth was it tasted of redemption.

LeCarre turned around to the small crowd of onlookers and emergency personnel standing nervously behind a pathetic cordon which would have done little to protect them from the blast.

'You're welcome!' he shouted, before taking his phone from his pocket and calling Detective Tim Rhodes.


'You did a good job, Roger. Thank you,' Chang said to LeCarre as she handed him back his badge. Three hours he'd been suspended, which is roughly four episodes of *Pointless*. 'I still want you to get some sleep.'

He was sober now but he wasn't ready to sleep. Not one drop of sleep until the culprit was behind bars and he'd successfully moved on to a new gas and electric tariff.

They were in Chang's glass cube of an office at Exeter Police Station. Earlier on that very week they'd been making passionate love on her desk, like two wild animals who had for some reason ended up in an office. Roger LeCarre and Beverley Chang were still connected by an electric lust, which coincidentally was the name of the band Roger had fronted as a teenager. With a blend of classic rock and competent funk, Electric Lust should have hit the big time but the music industry is all about who you know.

Had Electric Lust achieved the success they deserved, would Roger be where he was now? Most likely not. History suggests he'd have been dragged down into the whirlpool of drugs and tardy punctuality that comes with popular music. He was a highly decorated police officer, dammit, and *still* he'd spent the last few hours mashed up on Gasmask.

Never again.

*Never again.*

This last week he'd taken drugs and killed a man. By becoming a temporary criminal, he'd grown to understand criminals better. Know your enemy. It had made him a better police officer. Perhaps next week he'd go shoplifting.

A hand landed on his rugged knee – Chang's hand.

'You're the hero this city needs.'

Even with the fabric of his Antique Beige Cotton Traders ultimate chino trousers between them, he could feel Chang's raw half-Chinese sexuality pulsating into him.

No.

*No.*

His wife was in a coma and he had vowed to stay true to her. If Carrie died, then sure, he and Chang could dance the sex fandango again, possibly this weekend, but no, he had to be respectful to his spouse. He had to be a good husband.

But there was still something he needed to ask Chang about.

'DM Enterprises,' said LeCarre.

'I beg your pardon?' spluttered Chang.

'DM Enterprises. Tell me about it.'

'I don't know what you're talking about, Roger.'

'Oh, I think you do. The payments into your account,' said LeCarre, pinning Chang with his erotic yet enquiring gaze. 'When we were making love the other day –' Chang shifted in her chair, turned on by the memory '– my eyes fell on to one of your bank statements. DM Enterprises – what is it?'

'Roger, this is highly inappropriate.'

'I put a part of my body inside a part of yours on this very desk. Don't talk to me about inappropriate. I'm a detective. Allow me to do some detective work. It's what you pay me for, after all. DM Enterprises – is it Donkey Malone?'

'You're accusing me of taking money from Donkey Malone?'

'I'm not accusing you of anything. I'm just asking you a question. Pretend for a moment I'm Bradley Walsh and you're on *The Chase*.'

Roger had defused one bomb only to set another off in Chang's office.

'I'm not a dirty copper, Roger,' Chang said to LeCarre, who ironically was a dirty copper because, thinking about it, he hadn't had the time to wash since before he'd gone to New York.

'Glad to hear it. What's DM Enterprises?' Roger kept

repeating the question like a quizmaster on a particularly noisy Monday night at the Crown and Goose.

'You have no right to question me like this, Roger. I may have been under you the other day but professionally *you* are under *me*.'

'We're not allowed to get work on the side, Chang, and you know it. We're Devon and Cornwall police officers. Now, if this is something innocent then I'll say no more about it. But if you've been taking cash from the enemy, you'll have to use that cash to pay the price,' said Roger.

'I haven't been taking cash from the enemy,' said Chang, firmly, 'unless you see Martin Clunes as the enemy.'

LeCarre raised an eyebrow in reply. Martin Clunes?

'I take it you're familiar with the popular ITV comedy drama series *Doc Martin*?' said Chang.

'Of course,' said Roger. 'It's the pride of Cornwall, the jewel in their crown.'

'I've been doing some consultancy for them – West Country locations, police procedure, that sort of thing. It pays a little and, for your information, rule 229 of the Devon and Cornwall police force rulebook allows officers to do part-time work for ITV comedy dramas. Does that satisfy you, Detective? Or am I under arrest?'

'My apologies, ma'am.'

'That's all right, Roger,' said Chang. 'I'm just glad you're back on form.'

Chang understood that Detective Roger LeCarre was a maverick. It was his reckless search for the truth and nothing else, regardless of the consequences, that made him such a good copper.

'Where are you going now? To bed, I hope.'

LeCarre laughed loudly at the idea of going to bed. 'Will you be attending tonight, ma'am?'

'The opening ceremony for the Capital of Culture celebrations? The much-anticipated event where the whole of Exeter will be gathered to see the unveiling of Europe's largest Ferris wheel?'

'Yes.'

'Yes, I will. Will you, Roger?'

'Yes. Oh yes. Oh yes indeed.'

There it was, in LeCarre's voice, in his gait. Chang knew what the whole of Exeter would soon know. Tonight, with the taste of World War Two bomb wire still in his mouth, *Detective Roger LeCarre would be revealing the killer.*

# TWENTY-SEVEN

4.54 billion years ago, in a new solar system, a planet began its life. Chaotic volcanic activity birthed oceans. The first crust was formed. Through countless millennia, rocks were born, metals, minerals. Those substances would go on to become the raw materials which comprise our world. The present day: in a factory in what has come to be known as France, silica, soda, lime, dolomite, magnesium oxide and aluminium oxide were combined and placed into a glass furnace at 1,675 degrees Celsius. The substance was poured into moulds and distributed around Europe in the form of pint glasses. One such pint glass found itself on a table in the south-west of England in the Crown and Goose pub, Exeter. A hand grasped the receptacle. The hand belonged to a man who didn't merely understand the geological eons that had gone into every inch around him but who in every move he made, in every breath he took represented them. The man was Detective Roger LeCarre and he was on his third pint of Ruddles.

He had to be careful to monitor how much he drank. Tonight was important. Tonight was the night when justice would be served and Detective Roger LeCarre would be doing the serving. That was if everything went to plan.

Science teaches us that three pints is the level at which man performs at his best. LeCarre couldn't be sure but he suspected that three pints was the volume Usain Bolt had drunk before he ran 100 metres in a world record time of 9.58 seconds in 2009. LeCarre wouldn't have to run that fast tonight. Not if everything went to plan.

At 4.30 p.m. on a Friday afternoon, the Crown and Goose was quiet. The city's leading employers hadn't spat out their throng just yet. A certain kind of group of men were gathered – each on their own, each with their own burden, their own story to tell. Tonight, Detective Roger LeCarre would be writing another chapter of his own. That was if everything went to plan.

Pale and crystal malted barley, Bramling Cross hops. Bitter, yet with a light sweetness. The aroma made its way to his nasal passage, the beer to his lips and down his masculine throat. A younger LeCarre would not have had the sense to savour these moments, too caught up in climbing the greasy pole and online Scrabble. Roger had earned this brief pause. Could tonight be his final chapter? Not if everything went to plan.

If everything went to plan then tonight would be the first chapter in a new volume.

A door opened and five red-nosed men looked up from their respective corners to see the unmistakable frame of LeBron Jax. Six feet and four inches of Devonian muscle.

LeCarre nodded at Jax who nodded back, slowly, and went to the bar. A minute later he placed a fresh pint of Ruddles in front of LeCarre and sat opposite him with a Snowball, Jax's signature Advocaat-based drink.

The men didn't speak, just stared into each other's eyes, heterosexually. Forty minutes passed. The other customers drank, the barman cleaned glasses, the television quietly emitted an episode of ITV's hit daytime quiz show *Tipping Point*. Roger LeCarre and LeBron Jax didn't say a word, even when they desperately wanted to shout out answers to the frankly remedial questions.

They had to sort things out and this is how men, real men, resolved things: by staring at each other in a pub.

Jax was the first to break.

'Roger, I'm ...'

'Sorry?' said LeCarre, finishing Jax's sentence for him. 'I know. You had a damn affair with my damn wife. I should damn well hope you're damn sorry.'

'I am.'

'Good. Then let's say no more about it.'

And that was that. Forty minutes of staring, twenty seconds of talking and they were done. If all the leaders of the world could just sit down for a drink together in the Crown and Goose then maybe there could be an end to war. With a capacity of 220 people this would actually be a viable event. Not all the leaders would get a seat but surely it would be worth it? LeCarre made a mental note to get in touch with the UN at some point to propose it.

LeCarre and Jax clinked glasses. Their drinks were different colours and so was their skin but their blood was Devon and Cornwall Police blue and that was all that mattered.

'I need your help,' said LeCarre, for the first time in his life.

'I'm right here, buddy,' said Jax. 'LeCarre and Jax – the terrible twosome.'

'Threesome.'

'Threesome?'

The pub's clientele were looking at the door again. Someone else was entering the Crown and Goose. Yankee hat on his head, copy of the *New Yorker* in his hand, and whistling the theme tune to *Sex and the City*.

*Detective Tim Rhodes had had quite the few days.*

How many hours before had LeCarre called him and told him to come back from New York? Wasn't it that morning? Surely it didn't make sense that he was here in Exeter so quickly. Especially since Concorde, the only jet that could have feasibly got him across the Atlantic in that kind of time, took its last flight in October 2003.

The important thing was that Rhodes had *found a way*. Good police officers always *find a way* and Detective Tim Rhodes was proving to be a very good police officer indeed.

'How's Carrie?' asked Rhodes.

'Stable,' said LeCarre.

'A stable woman? That's a first!'

The three men laughed at Jax's casually misogynistic joke.

'Why did they shoot her?' asked Rhodes. 'Have you found out yet?'

Both of LeCarre's eyes narrowed. 'That gun wasn't aimed at Carrie, Rhodes. It was aimed at me. I'm the one who's chasing the killer. I'm the one they wanted to eliminate. Carrie was just a very unfortunate bystander.'

Silence, but for the gentle tones of Ben Shephard on the

television. A brief pause while the men contemplated the forces they were dealing with.

'Did you get what I asked?' said LeCarre.

'It's really quite incredible,' said Rhodes.

Rhodes pulled his 15-inch Dell laptop computer with Intel Celeron processor from his leather briefcase and showed Jax and LeCarre what he'd found. They had their killer. All they had to do now was catch them.

The three men talked through their roles for the evening over another drink. Everything that night had to work like a well-oiled machine: alcohol was the oil, the men were the machine.


Seven minutes past nine in the evening. Hundreds of legs, each in a pair, each attached to a person, were moving in the same direction – towards the giant stage which had been erected at the top of Exeter High Street. People of all ages, creeds, races, except for maybe Native American because statistically that just seemed unlikely.

The people of Exeter were glad to have something to celebrate. They sure needed it. Murders in the streets, a spiralling drugs war, the closure of Debenhams – these people had been through so much. They needed a break and Mayor Rufus Scallion was about to give it to them.

Detective Roger LeCarre eyed the hordes as he leaned against a ledge outside the Crown and Goose. He'd overshot his three-pint target by some distance. It didn't matter. Each sip of Ruddles trickled down his throat like a hoppy waterfall, refuelling him, getting him into The Zone. This was his Superbowl, his World Cup Final, his final round on *Pointless*. No second chances – he had to get it right. Someone out there wanted him dead, and yet . . .

He felt calm. He felt ready.

*But then.*

A thought struck him like a thunderbolt, like a taser to his solar plexus. How could he have been so stupid? How could he forget? Suddenly he was sweating like a packaged cheese. Everything was supposed to be in place. The whole night was like a house of cards – one false move and everything could fall apart.

Forget it, he told himself. Just put it to the back of your mind. What's done is done, or rather *not* done. You don't have time to fix it. The plan was about to commence. Everything had to be focused on the plan.

*But . . .*

His energy tariff expired at midnight that night. By 8 p.m. all the relevant call centres would be closed and the opportunity to change it in time would be gone. How could he maintain the required focus in the knowledge that in a matter of hours he'd be paying over the odds for gas and electricity? There was no way around it.

*He had to find a new energy provider and he had to do it now.*

LeCarre pulled out his Huawei P30 Pro and went straight to his most trusted comparison website. They were asking for details he didn't have to hand. How many kilowatts was he using? He didn't know, dammit! He was flying blind. How could he have let himself get so precariously close to a poor energy deal?

Scottish Power. A quick scan – far quicker than felt comfortable – suggested they had the best offer for Roger LeCarre's energy needs.

*Ring ring. Ring ring.*

Roger looked down at his Fitbit – 140 beats per minute.

'You're fourth in the queue. Your call is important to us.'

Is it? Maybe if they knew that this particular call was from a man who was about to save his city, it would be a little more important.

He could see the stage from where he was. Devon superstar Joss Stone would be performing soon. Who could forget her bestselling 2004 album *Mind, Body & Soul*? LeCarre's mind, body and soul would be in tatters if someone from Scottish Power didn't answer the phone soon.

'Hello, Scottish Power,' said the disconcertingly non-Scottish voice.

'Hello. My name is Detective Roger LeCarre and I need to change energy provider and I need to do it now.'

Detective Roger LeCarre could run a 5k in twenty-two minutes, he could cook a spaghetti bolognese in seventeen and he could rewire a standard British plug in four. That night he learned that he could change energy provider, saving himself a cool £38 a year, in two minutes and forty-five seconds flat – just in time for the arrival of Detectives LeBron Jax and Tim Rhodes, whose game of pool had come to an end.

It was time for their plan to commence.

LeCarre and Jax shook hands but in that cool way that some sportsmen do where their forearms are pointed upwards at a 45-degree angle, their biceps glistening in the setting sun.

'You ready to rock and roll?' said Jax.

'Brother, you know it.'

And they were brothers. It didn't matter that LeBron had been having an affair with Roger's wife. They were soldiers of the Devon and Cornwall police force, brothers in arms in the war against crime. That was what mattered.

'Professor.' LeCarre nodded at Rhodes. 'Is everything in place?'

'Everything is in place,' said Rhodes.

'Gatting and Hernandez?'

'They're in position,' said Rhodes.

LeCarre looked at Rhodes properly for the first time since Chang had introduced them in her office. A few days ago all he'd seen was a scrawny boffin, everything that was wrong with the way modern policing was headed – a guy more comfortable in a library than a ghetto. Now he saw a real copper and another brother.

'Good man,' said LeCarre as he gave Rhodes a heterosexual hug.

LeCarre sank the last of his Ruddles and set the glass down on the pub window ledge. The act was like pressing a button which set off a chain reaction. The three men moved in unison towards the festivities. Anyone watching might think they were accompanied by a soundtrack, such was their aura. It was as if they were moving in slow motion, and yet with purpose, a train of justice headed for their unsuspecting destination.

Joss Stone finished her song to rapturous applause and hugged Josh Widdicombe, the evening's master of ceremonies. Two children of Devon had returned home to bathe their West Country brethren in talent.

With that Jax, Rhodes and LeCarre, the trio, the three-pronged fork of justice, split and headed in different directions – Jax to the left, Rhodes to the right and Detective Roger LeCarre straight ahead, straight towards the stage, *straight towards the murderer.*

# TWENTY-EIGHT

Wikipedia tells us that Exeter has a population of 131,405, while Devon as a whole has 1,194,166 and Cornwall has 569,578. Anyone looking at the crowd that night might have thought that the whole of Devon and Cornwall's combined population of 1,763,744 were in attendance, although actually it was probably more like about 5,000.

After the events of the last few days, someone would have to edit those Wikipedia populations and subtract two – Charlie Fade and Sebastian Twine. Perhaps LeCarre would do it when he got home. *Right after he'd avenged their deaths.*

Or perhaps someone else might be editing Wikipedia instead and subtracting three.

By which I mean perhaps Roger LeCarre might die.

Although, obviously, babies are born all the time,

meaning if you wanted to do the job properly you'd have to add as well as subtract, so this whole premise is flawed.

Whatever the exact crowd size, the mood was jubilant – a carnival atmosphere. Exeter High Street looked like the Champs-Élysées on a celebratory night, except, instead of the Arc de Triomphe as its focal point, it had the John Lewis department store. Children sat on their fathers' shoulders craning for a glimpse of Josh Widdicombe. Given an opportunity to show pride in their city, people had taken it upon themselves to wear costumes. Some were dressed as Exeter Cathedral, some as the Princesshay Shopping Centre. LeCarre must have spotted at least fifty 'Chris Martin from Coldplays', although it was possible that some of them were men who just happened to be wearing jeans and T-shirt. '*Semper fidelis*' was everywhere. On homemade banners, tattooed on to people's arms, etched into people's faces. Exeter's motto meant something to these people.

*Little did they know it meant murder.*

Directly in front of the stage was a roped-off VIP area guarded by police. Societies have always found a way to delineate status. Even the *supposed* equal societies of Mao's China and the Soviet Union had elites. Exeter was no different and the city's finest, such as Kelly and Baz from

Radio Exe's breakfast show, were kept safely away from their public.

Detective Roger LeCarre detested such inequalities. If he had it his way, the entire world would be equal except for maybe at Alton Towers, where the offer to buy a Fastrack Pass, allowing you to jump queues, was an excellent option for those with extra cash and young families.

LeCarre flashed his reacquired badge at PC Mohammed Flintoff. The first time they'd crossed paths, Flintoff had lifted a police cordon for LeCarre, allowing him to enter Charlie Fade's crime scene. Now Flintoff was lifting a velvet rope. The moment, which seemed to bookend the week, provided a pleasing symmetry, worthy of a first-class novel.

Chief Superintendent Beverley Chang was there, in tight-fitting leather trousers and high heels, watching the stage and flinging her shapely head back in howls of erotic laughter at Josh Widdicombe's observational riffing. Chang was ignorant of LeCarre's plan but that wouldn't last long. Soon the whole world, or at least those with access to South-West regional news, would know.

Junior Lamb had somehow talked his way into the enclosure, snooker cue by his side, as always. Roger inhaled a familiar scent and turned to see Melanie Fade watching the entertainment. She looked just as good as she had the day first they met, five days ago, when he'd told her that her son was dead and then had sex with her.

As he made his way closer to the giant platform stage, Roger found himself walking through a cloud of Cuban cigar smoke. Donkey Malone. The king of the underworld would have had no trouble getting into the VIP section. Throughout history, elites had always enjoyed rubbing shoulders with stars from the criminal class and Donkey was a man happy to take advantage. Ordinarily, the sight of Malone in respectable company would have sickened LeCarre, but tonight was different.

It was all part of the plan. Malone was *supposed* to be there. *They all were.*

The evening air was filled with the sound of five thousand Devonians laughing courtesy of a Josh Widdicombe routine about service stations. Had LeCarre been listening he might have been laughing too, but right now he was focused on his route.

Either side of the platform were steps leading to the stage, each guarded by a large security guard. If LeCarre were lucky, his badge would be enough to get him through, but he wasn't willing to rely on luck. If Jax had done as promised then the guard to LeCarre's right would have already been told to let LeCarre by. Roger looked at him to see if he could catch his eye – a simple nod could steady the detective's nerves – but the guard just stared straight ahead.

It wasn't quite time yet. But the moment was seconds away.

What if the guard hadn't been tipped off? What if there was a delay and Chang stepped in and stopped it? Or one of the killer's goons? Roger could be erased in minutes. Another victim. Another grain of sand washed from the shore by the giant wave of crime.

Roger checked his Fitbit – 280 beats per minute.

The laugher turned to applause. Josh Widdicombe's superbly crafted routine was at an end. Would applause turn to mayhem? Only time would tell. LeCarre was about to plunge into the water of truth without knowing the temperature.

'And now, ladies and gentlemen,' said the relatively wealthy observational comedian, 'it is my great honour to welcome to the stage the man who made all of this happen, the reason why we're all here tonight. Exeter! I give you your mayor – Mr Rufus Scallion!'

Between them Joss Stone and Josh Widdicombe have two Brit Awards, one Grammy and a Chortle Award nomination, but the adulation the crowd had given them was nothing compared to what it gave Rufus Scallion. The tubby mayor soaked up the cheers, waving to the masses as he approached the microphone, once again in his customary full ceremonial outfit. Few politicians get to experience such moments and those that do tend to go on to commit genocide.

As Scallion was making his way to the microphone, Detective Roger LeCarre was heading towards the large red-headed security guard on his right and the steps that led to the stage.

'I believe you're expecting me,' said LeCarre.

'Any friend of LeBron Jax is a friend of mine,' said the redhead, and LeCarre was through.

Good old Jax. Beverley Chang's Botoxed face somehow managed a frown as she spotted LeCarre walking up the steps towards the front of the stage.

'Please. Please . . . ' Scallion was gesturing for the crowd to quieten down their applause but it was clear he was quite happy for it to continue. Soon their attention would be on the Ferris wheel and not him. Why not bathe in their love for a few seconds more?

A twitch in Scallion's eye. Whatever Roger LeCarre's plan was, what the mayor saw wasn't part of his. The handsome detective, his back to the crowd, was moving towards Scallion.

LeCarre could see Scallion quickly assessing the

situation. Why was the man he'd made Exeter's Person of the Year just five days ago walking across the stage towards him, right in the middle of his big moment? Had something happened? A terrorist threat? Or something else? It couldn't be. Could it?

Had yesterday's bullet's trajectory been just a few inches different then LeCarre wouldn't be walking at all.

*Because dead men can't walk.*

Scallion covered the Sennheiser microphone with his hand and spoke. 'Detective LeCarre. Is there something . . . ?'

'I'm sorry, Mr Mayor. I'm going to have to take the Sennheiser microphone for a moment.'

'Absolutely not. Can't this wait? I have a Ferris wheel to unveil, a Capital of Culture to celebrate.'

LeCarre pinned Scallion with his eyes. It was a look which said he meant business – like someone registering their company with Companies House.

'Step aside, Mayor.'

Scallion did as he was told and LeCarre stepped up to the microphone. LeBron, watching from the wings, said a little prayer for his former partner. This was it. The biggest moment of LeCarre's career and LeBron had a front-row seat, although technically he was actually standing.

'Testing. Testing. One. Two.' LeCarre looked out over

the sea of people. How would they take what he had to say? He could be in for choppy waters.

The truth, he told himself. People respect the truth.

'Hello. I'm sorry to interrupt this evening's entertainment. My name is Detective Roger LeCarre. Sorry, can I ask someone in the sound booth ... I'm sounding a little reverby ... thank you. My name is Detective Roger LeCarre. Last Sunday I won Exeter's Person of the Year but that's not important. It was on BBC *Spotlight* and I think there was an article on it in the *Express & Echo*. Also, I don't know if you heard about the World War Two bomb earlier on today? The one that a man defused with his teeth? Well, that man was me. Anyway, like I say, not important. Just trying to give you a little background info.

'I'm here to talk about two young men who lost their lives this past week. Both of them in this city centre, this city centre we all love so much. Charlie Fade was murdered not far from here, beside St Pancras Church in the Guildhall Shopping Centre, last Saturday night. I was tasked with finding his killer. Just two days later, Sebastian Twine, another young man, soon to be a father – a man who knew who killed Charlie Fade – was stabbed, then pushed to his death from the John Lewis café behind where I stand this very moment.'

'Is Joss Stone coming back on?' shouted someone from the crowd. 'She didn't do "You Had Me". I love that song.'

'I don't know. I think she's concentrating on her newer stuff now,' said LeCarre. 'Please allow me to finish and then you can all enjoy the rest of your night.'

LeCarre squinted. The Devon sun was setting. Soon it would be dark. Where did the sun go at night? No one knew. Now Detective Roger LeCarre was shining a light, shining a light on the events of the past week.

'Charlie Fade was a nineteen-year-old kid who made some bad choices and walked straight into the jaws of the biggest cat in town, Donkey Malone. Big mistake. Fade was dealing a new drug by the name of Gasmask for Malone, to fund his own dirty habit. But Charlie Fade wasn't your average drug dealer: Fade had a big mouth and a conscience – bad combination. Some things go together. Southern Comfort and lemonade, for example. Not a big mouth and a conscience. Not in this town ... '

'Where's the Ferris wheel?'

'We want Joss Stone back!'

'Seriously, if you keep interrupting me, it's only going to take longer. Give me a minute and I promise I will get to the point.'

LeCarre cleared his throat. Better than someone slitting

it. At least he'd got this far. Who knew what powers he was messing with on that stage in Exeter that night? He gripped the microphone stand with one clammy hand and continued.

'Gasmask is a dangerous drug. It can make a person do some pretty wild things. I'm ashamed to say I found that out for myself this week. At one stage I started dancing to my wife's life-support machine. Actually, there's probably still some of it in my system. I'm babbling. The Devon and Cornwall police force prides itself on knowing things – that's why we have the most consistent pub quiz team in the south-west – but until a few hours ago we didn't know where the Gasmask that's flooding this city was coming from. All we knew was that it was killing it. Charlie Fade knew and Charlie Fade started talking. That's why Charlie Fade had to be killed.'

'Where was the Gasmask coming from, Detective LeCarre?' shouted a young girl on her dad's shoulders.

'Good question. Glad you're all paying attention now. This is good. This is good. Right, where was the Gasmask coming from? New York City. Except they didn't call it Gasmask. They called it Dalliance. Different name, same drug. A little like how they say "elevator" instead of "lift". So, Donkey Malone killed Charlie Fade, right? Donkey

Malone was the one running the Exeter drug trade and he couldn't have a young pup yapping in the Rainbow Snooker Club about where his precious Gasmask was coming from so he put him down. Wrong.'

LeCarre looked down at Donkey who, like everyone else in the VIP enclosure, was listening intently.

'You're a big cheese in Devon, Donkey, but you're not a transatlantic cheese. You're a Ticklemore. You're no Cheddar. Donkey Malone didn't have the connections to open up a drug trade route between New York and Exeter. But someone else did – Mayor Rufus Scallion.'

A huge gasp from the crowd. The mayor shifted from one foot to the other and looked for an exit. As he moved he was hit by a shard of light, a spotlight from high up in the lighting gallery.

'There are two snipers trained on you, Mayor Scallion,' said LeCarre. 'You know about snipers, don't you, Mayor? Move from that spotlight and one of my colleagues, Hernandez or Gatting, the two finest shots south of Tiverton, will put a bullet through one of your vital organs. You want a bullet through one of your vital organs, do you, Mayor? Well, do ya? Do ya?'

Scallion shook his head.

'Good. Neither did my wife,' said LeCarre. 'And I'm not

done talking yet. Earlier on today, I was thinking about nature ...'

'Is this going to take long?' said a woman in the crowd. 'We've only booked the babysitter until ten.'

'Seriously, if everyone just lets me talk then it will all be over a lot quicker. Nature. I was stood by the Trews Weir and I was thinking about nature and how man tries to control it. A city is a piece of nature, it is an organism, impossible to master. Our mayor thought he could master it. Thought he could control nature to his own benefit. He was wrong.

'Being mayor of a global powerhouse doesn't just come with gold chains and a happy flow of roasted chicken legs, it comes with diplomatic benefits. Rufus Scallion has been using his diplomatic powers to traffic Gasmask into the ghettos of Exeter, Tiverton and Barnstaple for a while now. The question is why? Evil people don't think they're evil. That's why. Rufus Scallion thought by obtaining Gasmask for Donkey Malone to sell and taking a cut for Exeter City Council he was doing good. Remember that new pelican crossing on Priory Road? The statue of Chris Martin in Anders Square? The adventure playground in Tipton Park? Ever wondered how Exeter was paying for all this stuff without so much as a one per cent council tax rise? The sad truth is that our beloved mayor paid for all of that with drug money, laundered through the Rainbow Snooker Club. My partner Rhodes, a computer whizz with a degree from Leicester De Montfort University, a man I underestimated but now love and respect in an entirely platonic way, was able to obtain the records through a process known as "hacking". Scallion told himself he was doing it all for his city. Meanwhile, he was blind to the fact he was killing it. Scallion thought he was the dam controlling the river. Instead, he was the flood. Perhaps the adulation helped. The people love you, Rufus, or at least they did until earlier on in this paragraph. You needed that love. You fed off it. And you wanted more. That's where the Ferris wheel came in.'

LeCarre dramatically pulled a giant red lever beside him, a 150-metre high curtain fell and the already-spinning Ferris wheel, standing where the Streamers party shop used to be, was revealed.

'Isn't that magnificent?' said LeCarre. 'I'm sorry, Scallion. I know you wanted to be the one who pulled that lever. Murderers don't get to pull levers. Not on my watch. To be fair, we've all seen it already. I mean, they've been building it all week. One week to build the biggest Ferris wheel in Europe. Not bad. A man with an ego as big as yours needed

241

a Ferris wheel to match, didn't he? Shame you had to do what you did to get it.'

LeCarre turned to the crowd again. His nerves had gone. He felt at home on a stage. Finally he was fulfilling the early promise he'd shown in his school's production of *Guys and Dolls*.

'Once our mayor had the idea for a giant Ferris wheel, it didn't leave his mind. It turned and turned around your massive brain, didn't it, Scallion? Well, it's been turning around mine, too. Rufus Scallion had a right-hand man and his name was Sebastian Twine. Remember him? The one who got pushed off John Lewis? A little while ago, Scallion sent Twine to New York to arrange a much bigger order of Gasmask, bigger than ever before, big enough to fund a Ferris wheel once it had been sold in the Devon ghettos. All went well. My partner, Detective Tim Rhodes, was able to establish that in New York. Twine even got a nice new scarf for his wife. You see, Scallion would have you believe that Twine was just a junkie, another lost soul, but Twine was a very together young man. Sure, he liked indie music and poetry slams but he didn't like taking drugs. Maybe he had his eyes set on the top job one day. Maybe you didn't like that, Rufus. Anyway, it was back in Exeter that everything went wrong. Twine knew that he was involved in something rotten. It was a compromise he was prepared to make – politics is a dirty game. What he couldn't stomach was murder, and when Sebastian Twine saw Rufus Scallion murder Charlie Fade right outside St Pancras Church, that's when his conscience came in to play.

'Do you remember when we first met, Scallion? On Sunday night? You were announcing me as Exeter Person of the Year in our glorious castle. I know why you gave me that award. You wanted to make an ally of me. Well, that's one thing you can't buy. You may be able to buy as many drugs as you like in this town but you can't buy Detective Roger LeCarre. All giving me that award did was tell Sebastian Twine who the best cop in town was. That's why he was going to tell me you killed Charlie Fade and *that* is why you killed Sebastian Twine before he could. I hope you rot in prison, Rufus Scallion, I really do.'

The mayor had stayed quiet throughout LeCarre's speech. Telling a man he has a couple of snipers aimed at him is a very effective way of shutting him up.

*But now that man had something to say.*

'Very good, Detective. A very good story indeed. Worthy of Exeter University alumnus J.K. Rowling. But I'm afraid, like Ms Rowling's, your story is fiction. If you had anything approaching proof, I think we'd have heard it by now.'

243

'Rhodes!' said LeCarre.

Something changed and five thousand people tilted their heads up to the giant screen above LeCarre and Scallion.

'This is CCTV footage of the murder of Charlie Fade,' said LeCarre.

'Do we really have to watch this?' shouted the man with a child on his shoulders.

'Sorry,' said LeCarre. 'I didn't think about that. Cover her eyes? Yeah, everyone with kids, cover their eyes.'

Scallion wanted to cover his but he had to look.

'Surprised, mayor?' glinted LeCarre.

The footage was grainy but everything was clear enough. LeBron Jax watched from backstage and winced as the video showed he and Carrie walking, arm in arm, across the square. Then each of the other suspects going about their business could be seen. Melanie Fade walked across. Then Josh Widdicombe, bathed in a post-gig glow, then Donkey Malone, then Beverley Chang, then Junior Lamb, snooker cue in hand. Each of them had something to do with their Saturday night, but it wasn't murder.

'Sorry, can you fast-forward a bit, Rhodes? All of this is irrelevant,' said LeCarre.

Rhodes skipped ahead until they saw Charlie Fade. A skinny kid with nothing but a KFC Tower Burger and a mayor walking towards him. Scallion came from the shadows. To a kid like Fade, who didn't keep up with the news, who wouldn't have recognised his mayor, Scallion must have looked like a stray from a stag do. His velvet robes, his triangular hat, his chains, it must have looked like a costume. But it was all very real, not least the giant sword Scallion took from his hip and plunged into Fade.

'Quite the brazen move, Mayor,' said LeCarre. 'Doing it out in the open. I guess you figured by St Pancras Church was a quiet spot and by this point you were so manic with power you thought you could get away with anything.'

It was only when they saw Scallion twist the blade that the crowd really began to flinch. Have you ever seen five thousand people flinch? All at once? It's quite the sight. They watched through their fingers as the video showed Scallion carving SEMPER FIDELIS into Fade's chest.

'*Semper fidelis.* You told yourself you were doing it for Exeter. But look what Exeter thinks of you now.'

Scallion looked out at an ocean of disgusted faces.

'Our mayor thought he'd successfully turned all the CCTV cameras away that night. But there was one he missed. Sebastian Twine had the tape and he was going to give it to me before Mayor Scallion killed him. My partner Rhodes was able to retrieve this from something called the

Cloud. The next cloud you'll be seeing, Scallion, will be from an exercise yard in one of Her Majesty's prisons.

'We don't have any footage of Twine's murder, I'm afraid. You successfully avoided the camera that time, Scallion. But I can still prove you did it. Jax!'

LeBron Jax entered, stage left, dragging the body of Sebastian Twine.

'Jesus Christ!' someone said from the crowd. 'This is getting proper mental.'

LeCarre turned to Twine's grieving widow, who was standing in the VIP section next to Junior Lamb and his snooker cue. 'I'm sorry, Caroline, it's the only way I could get justice for your husband.'

Jax rested the four-day-old corpse between LeCarre and Scallion and gave Roger another cool, manly, sky-pointing handshake.

'Excuse me a moment, Mayor,' said LeCarre. 'You have something I'd like to borrow, if I may. My old buddy LeBron Jax, the finest cop I know, today went and retrieved the body of Sebastian Twine so I could prove you killed him.'

LeCarre took Scallion's sword from the scabbard on his hip. The mayor was too stunned to stop him.

'This –' LeCarre held the sword up to the crowd '– is the sword your mayor killed Charlie Fade with and I can prove to you all now that it is the very same sword that he used to murder Sebastian Twine.'

LeCarre, in a move worthy of his status as the south-west's number one maverick copper, carefully drove the sword straight into Sebastian Twine's body.

'Ladies and gentlemen, I am now placing the mayor's sword directly into the wound which he gave to Sebastian Twine before he pushed him from the John Lewis café. And would you look at that? *It fits perfectly.* It's an unusual wound, made by an unusual blade, wielded by a *very* unusual politician.' Then LeCarre improvised his own twist on the famous Johnnie Cochran line. 'If the sword fits, the mayor's a shit.'

'Scallion knew that, unless he stopped me, I'd catch him eventually. That's why he took a shot at me yesterday, but instead hit my beautiful wife Carrie LeCarre. Too bad, Mayor. I'd say it's time to go back to the shooting range but there are no shooting ranges *in prison*. I think there's a phrase for moments like these. Case closed.'

'Very good, Detective,' said Scallion in resignation. 'I couldn't have hoped for a better adversary. You're a very smart man, a credit to your quiz team. But I wonder if you're quite as smart as you think you are.'

LeCarre raised an eyebrow.

'I don't know who took a shot at you, LeCarre, but it sure wasn't me.'

'Of course it was you, Scallion. Enough of your politician's lies!'

'Detective, you're disappointing me,' said Scallion. 'I have a very clear method. Stabbing with the sword, followed by carving *semper fidelis* into the corpse. Of course, this is your field of expertise, not mine, but don't you think firing at you with a sniper rifle goes rather against my modus operandi?'

'He's got a point,' mumbled a girl on her dad's shoulders.

The reality hit LeCarre and the crowd at the same time.

'It would appear I'm not the only man in Exeter who wants you dead, LeCarre,' said Scallion.

Who? The answer came quicker than anyone expected. LeCarre watched LeBron run to the edge of the stage and leap into the VIP enclosure. Junior Lamb was raising his snooker cue and aiming it directly at Detective Roger LeCarre. Before he could shoot, the Virgin Active-maintained body of Detective LeBron Jax was on top of him and grabbing hold of the cue. Jax looked at the cue, then held it up to LeCarre.

'Adapted into a bolt-action Remington sniper rifle,' said Jax. 'Best snooker-cue-into-a-rifle job I've seen in a while.'

'Why, Junior?' said LeCarre, in sorrow. 'Why?'

'You're the reason I don't have a dad,' said Junior. 'You weren't there.'

'Junior . . . Zizzi's . . . calzone . . . ' LeCarre was struggling to comprehend the enormity of the events that seemed to keep on unfolding like some kind of endless umbrella. 'Junior, I'm sorry. I should have been there, I know.'

With LeCarre dumbfounded at finding himself in the act of apologising to the person who shot his wife, Scallion took his chance to escape.

*Now or never.*

The mayor ran not for backstage, not for the crowd that once loved him, but for the spinning Ferris wheel his evil had funded, the speed and suddenness of his move taking the distracted snipers by surprise. He leapt on to the helicopter-like landing gear of one of its impressively slick capsules and it took him up, up towards the evening sky.

For years people would wonder why LeCarre did what he did in that moment. LeCarre could never explain it. 'Caught up in the excitement, I guess,' he'd say. He did what he did and that was that. Rather than simply waiting for the wheel to come back round again, and arresting Scallion at the bottom, LeCarre leapt on to the next capsule and dangerously hung from its landing gear.

The two men were engaged in a mid-air battle and, now

that he had climbed on top of his own capsule, which sat below Scallion's, Roger LeCarre was at a disadvantage. Scallion threw one of his giant golden chains into LeCarre's face, centuries of Exeter history nearly knocking him 100 metres to the ground. Hernandez and Gatting and their sniper guns could do nothing. Directly behind the wheel was the St Cuthbert's School Choir, due to sing the national anthem. Scallion was a moving target. Miss him and you were likely to hit a promising young chorister.

This was between LeCarre and Scallion. No one else.

LeCarre made a jump for Scallion's capsule and just about made it. The wheel was reaching its peak. Until the adventures of this week, Roger had been running 10k a day. It's amazing how quickly your fitness can drop off, he thought, puffing. Now he had to clamber to join Scallion on the top of his capsule, while taking more chains to the face, as what seemed like the whole of Exeter watched. 'Do it for Devon,' he grunted to himself, as he somehow got face to face with Scallion just as the capsule made it to the Ferris wheel's apex, 150 metres above the ground.

Now that they were on equal terms, it was no fair fight. LeCarre was the younger, fitter man and he had the whole city behind him. Scallion swung for him, wildly, but LeCarre's reflexes were quick. He ducked the punch, hit

Scallion in his mighty gut, then landed a left hook on his square-shaped face.

'Goodnight, mayor. Nightmare. *Good. Night. Mayor*,' said LeCarre, relatively happy with the pun he'd managed to come up with in high-pressure circumstances.

The children who dared watch got a science lesson that night. How fast does a mayor tumble 150 metres? Fast. Very fast.

Scallion had killed two people that week and, as he hit the ground, Detective Roger LeCarre joined him in that miserable feat. He never did get to see the mayor in handcuffs, but he did get justice. Of that there was no doubt.

# TWENTY-NINE

'Get some sleep,' Chang had said, as they threw Scallion's body parts into the van.

'Ha ha ha ha ha ha ha ha.' LeCarre had laughed, like he was listening to *Up with Kelly and Baz* on Radio Exe. 'I've got places to be.'

And he had.

*Bleep. Bleep. Bleep.*

Detective Roger LeCarre looked at his wife. He'd remember this week for the rest of his life. If he ever took the time to write it down it would make a really good book. The bandages on her face had been removed by the doctors. She was as beautiful as ever but, with her face as it was, not in a conventional sense – more in the way that an abstract painting is beautiful, or a well put-together fish pie.

Carrie was still unconscious so LeCarre was able to speak to her without her saying anything back. It was like the early years of their relationship. They'd stay up for hours, right through the night, LeCarre just talking and talking – telling her about his childhood, about the history of the British road network and about why James Dyson's true talent was actually self-promotion rather than engineering and many of his so-called inventions were actually overrated pieces of tat. Good times.

'Carrie . . . *j'adore tu*. I really really do, *j'adore tu*. I know sometimes I may not have shown it. All those days I made a sandwich and didn't clean up after myself. Silly little things like not replacing a toilet roll when I'd finished it or that time I moved to Falmouth for six months with another woman. In my defence, I leave the sandwich stuff out in case you want to make a sandwich for yourself – I'm *trying* to be considerate – but I do appreciate that over the years these things have accumulated and damaged our marriage.

'I need you to understand that . . . *I get it now*. Things are going to be different from now on. I'm going to be a better husband to you and a better father to Destiny. Hey, when this all blows over, when you're back to your best, we should all take a holiday – Center Parcs. Dammit, I'll book us a luxury treehouse. Why not? We deserve it. It won't be cheap but I can shift things around a bit. I sorted out the energy tariff, by the way – the savings might pay for it on their own. You, me, Destiny, we can have a little family archery competition – but I do want to stress, I think we should all play by the same rules. If we let Destiny stand closer we're just teaching her to fail.

'Carrie, I want us to be a family again. I just need you to focus on getting better. Technically, it's possible that I'm talking to a vegetable, in which case this speech is completely redundant and I should think about moving on with my life, but if you can hear me in there, Carrie, I need you to know that I love you, Carrie LeCarre, and I always will, within reason.'

*Bleep. Bleep. Bleep.*

And then another sound. A different sound. Out of nowhere. Like a distant crow.

'Uuuugggggghhhh.'

'Carrie?'

'Uuuuuuugggggghhhh.'

'Carrie, you heard me?'

'Roooooggggggeeeeerrr.'

'Carrie, darling, it's so good to hear your voice again.'

'Roger, there's something . . . ' she strained.

'Yes, darling?'

'There's something I want you to do for me, before you go.' Every word was a struggle, but Carrie had something she simply had to say.

'What is it, darling? Anything, absolutely anything.'

*'Make love to me.'*


Roger had never made love to a woman who'd just woken up from a coma before. He'd been close a couple of times but the stars had never quite aligned. Now his wife was asking for a conjugal visit, right there and then, and he felt a responsibility to oblige.

Detective Roger LeCarre sanitised his hands and climbed on top of his wife. Home. It felt like home. These last few years he'd been floating around on the breeze. A night in Plymstock here, a night in Saltash there. A wayward warrior. This, this is where he belonged. On top of his wife. Unless she fancied going on top, which seemed unlikely under the circumstances.

Roger entered her, like he'd done so many times before. Like a train easing into Exeter St David's station, right on time. LeCarre was still wild with carnal lust for his recently shot wife.

'Do me, Roger. Yes, do me.'

Do her he did. The steady bleeps of her life-support

machine offered a helpful metronome to their lovemaking. It was like medical science itself approved. Once again they were just two people in love, doing the most natural thing in the world, having penetrative sex in the ICU at the Royal Devon and Exeter Hospital.

Detective LeCarre tenderly ejaculated into his wife, then went to see a friend.

'He's beautiful. He must get it from his mother,' LeCarre said, mock-punching Rhodes's arm, which held his newborn baby, who'd come into the world forty-two minutes after Scallion had died, neatly keeping Exeter's population exactly the same. The joshing was gentle now. Respectful. Kelly and Baz weren't the only partnership in town.

LeCarre and Jax's partnership was over. Jax saving LeCarre's life had been a nice note to end on. After what had happened with Carrie, they couldn't go back to the way things had been, but they had buried the pain right where men were supposed to – deep inside themselves. For the first time, LeCarre had managed to lose a partner without them dying and that was a kind of progress, he guessed. They'd still have their nights at the Crown and Goose. The Enforcers would continue and, with Detective Tim Rhodes in the quiz team, they'd be unstoppable.

'You got a name yet?' asked LeCarre.

'Roger. We're calling him Roger. Roger Rhodes.'

Detective Roger LeCarre wanted to cry but he couldn't. The week's escapades had drained his body entirely of liquid. He had nothing left. But he'd be back. He always was.

The men hugged heterosexually and Roger left Roger for some skin time with his father.


LeCarre pressed the up arrow beside the lift. One more stop before he finally headed home to rest his weary body on his memory-foam mattress. On the top floor, he found a fire escape and climbed the stairs to the hospital's roof. Atop the Ferris wheel he hadn't taken a moment to look at the view. I guess I was busy, he thought to himself. But now he had the chance to look out over Exeter.

*His city.*

He hadn't rid it of crime. Maybe he never would. But that wouldn't stop him trying.

Then he went to the sixth floor and bought a KitKat Chunky from the vending machine.

### THE END.

# ACKNOWLEDGEMENTS

Writing acknowledgements for a book like this feels a little grandiose, but not writing them feels ungrateful so I'm opting for the former.

Thank you to all at Sphere Books and Little, Brown: Thalia Proctor, Millie Seaward, Lucie Sharpe and, most especially, Ed Wood who patiently guided me, a novice and ignoramus, through the process of writing a book. Ed was able to help shape the story, encourage me and also pull me back from a couple of sentences which would have almost certainly got me cancelled.

Thank you to all at Curtis Brown, especially Gordon Wise and Sarah MacCormick. This project presented a series of unusual problems which they were able to valiantly overcome/recklessly overlook.

Huge thanks to the great Mark Billingham who got in

touch on Twitter and got everything rolling by introducing Detective Roger LeCarre to his publisher.

The Twitter community is a collection of the most appalling people humanity has ever produced, and yet, without their continued enthusiasm and encouragement, this absurd book would not have happened. So thank you, particularly to those Exeter locals who gave me vital scraps of detail.

Thank you to Dave Watson who suggested a Kia Ceed.

Huge thanks to Paul Doolan, who over two long phone calls and three long pub sessions talked through the whole book with me. Amongst other things, Paul suggested the name 'Gasmask'.

Thanks to my parents because it's always good to thank one's parents even if it's at the back of a book containing a number of grotesquely detailed sex scenes.

Finally, thanks to Laurie and Louis, although Louis is four so his contribution was minimal.